Kim—
Thank you so much for coming out & supporting me. I appreciate it SO MUCH.
Love you much ♡ Jeff

FIGHTING

DEMONS

3

T.C. FLENOID

Fighting Demons 3 © 2017 T.C.Flenoid

All rights reserved. No part of this book may be reproduced in any form or by any means without prior consent of the owner, excepting brief quotes used in interviews.

This is a work of fiction. Any references or similarities to actual events, real people, living or dead, is entirely coincidental.

First in print: May 2017
Cover Model: Bria J. Hill
Cover Design: 321Images-Karon Flenoid

ISBD-13: 978-1542547383
ISBN-10: 1542547385

This is for my G-mama, who I know is smiling down on all of us.
Love you always!

ACKNOWLEDGEMENTS

I thank God and give Him the glory! Without Him, none of what I have accomplished would be possible. I want to thank my husband, my creative partner in crime, for always supporting me and helping to make my dreams reality. It's been a long journey together, and I can't wait to see the success that the future holds for us. Keion, Elijah and Trinity, you three are my driving force. I pray constantly that I'm the kind of mother that you're able to be proud of... and even brag about a little bit. ☺ To my mama, thank you so much for your love and support. I'm so overly proud of all that YOU have accomplished! My beautiful, talented big, lil' sister, it's an honor watching you grow into your own creative self. You are amazing and I know you're destined to be great! To the rest of my FAM... even though we don't see each other as often as we'd like, know that I love y'all and you're never far from my thoughts! My boos, Jeek, Jessica, Keytra, Farren (ayo Bass!) KimmyP, Endea, and Shonda... love y'all! A huge thank you to my editors Dezell and Stacy, for the input, support and extra eyes! Stacy, I know I gave you a hard time, but you got me RIGHT lol! To everyone who loves me and supports my dream, you have my most gracious gratitude. THANK YOU!

1 Peter 4:10- Each of you has received a gift to use to serve others. Be good servants of God's various gifts of grace.

FIGURE OUT WHAT YOU LOVE TO DO, AND DO IT!!

PROLOGUE

I didn't expect that visiting my mama's ex best friend in prison would lead to her tellin' me that my man was behind all the nonsense that had been happening for the past few months. At first, I had hopes that Tasha was lying, trying to get back at me because I had never forgiven her for setting my mama up. After I showed her the picture of Derrick and she nodded, a part of me wanted to believe that, to her, he was just a random dude with dreads, and that she said she'd been working with him simply because she thought it would get me riled up. As I drove, though, the anxiety bubbled up in my chest. I knew she wasn't lying.

"Open the door, Derrick!!" I yelled as I pounded. He swung the door open and glared at me.

"Lea why you knockin' like the police?!" I pushed him backwards into the apartment and slammed the door.

"Nigga, you had my car windows and my house windows busted out, you broke into my house *twice*, sending me letters in the mail and shit, paintin' bullshit on my walls, had my tires slashed..." I kept moving forward while he kept stepping back. "What in the hell is your problem wit' me?" I half expected him to deny everything. This fool actually started *laughing*! I had to check myself and stop moving towards him. It finally hit me that he was probably crazy as hell.

"Who was it?" he asked calmly. I stared at him in disbelief. "Was it Tasha, or that crackhead, Theresa?" My mouth flew open. "You seem confused, baby. Let me clear some things up for you." He threw out his hand like he wanted me to shake it, and I jumped back. "Hi, I'm Anthony Merritt." I had to pause for a minute before I spoke again.

"I don't give a damn!" I yelled, tryin' to act like I wasn't scared shitless. Not only had the man I had been in a relationship with been terrorizing me and my son, but apparently his name wasn't even Derrick! I didn't know what the hell was goin' on, but I was kickin' myself for not picking my best friend, Mesha, up on my way there. I was alone with the nutcase.

"That name don't mean nothin' to you?!" he boomed, making me jump. I thought about the scholarships he had supposedly help me set up in my son's father's name.

"I want my ten thousand dollars back-"

"*Christopher Merritt*!!" It seemed like he screamed as loud as he could. The name bounced off my eardrums and I had to take a step back. I searched his face for any resemblance at all. When I saw it, I almost broke down. It was all in the eyes, one of those things you can't see until it's brought to your attention. How could I, of all people, have not noticed? How the hell could I have let him in my life and not realized at all that he resembled the man who had murdered my mama?! "You had my brother locked up for killin' that lil' bitch!" My breath stopped short in my throat. His *brother*... "Didn't have no damn daddy. *He* was my daddy! Yo' mama was a hoe, and she had my brother fucked up." The look in his eyes was psychotic. "She left him in that alley and she deserved what the fuck she got." I lost all the sense I had. His brother, Chris, had murdered my mama for lashing out at him when *he* was the one who had assaulted *her*! And Derrick had the audacity to be mad at *me*?! I lunged at his big ass. He grabbed me and threw me to the floor with ease.

"Fuck you!" I screamed.

"Already did that." He kicked me twice in my side and I folded over in pain. "Coulda got a lot more ass and money if those lil' stupid hoes hadn't ratted me out. But that's what I get. Guess all you simple bitches roll together huh?" He drug me by my hair and I screamed bloody murder, praying one of his neighbors would hear me. "He let me go and punched me dead in the mouth. "Shut the fuck up! Don't nobody wanna hear that!" I tasted blood and felt tears sliding down my face. "It would be so easy to kill you right now, but since I didn't get to have enough fun wit'chu, I'mma do that first." I couldn't help but think about what my daddy said. All those damn signs I thought I was seeing were just figments of my imagination. Lil Rell's face flashed before my eyes and I whimpered, wondering if I'd ever see my son again. I could fight back all I wanted but Derrick... *Anthony*... was obviously physically stronger than me. I figured that if I was about to die, there was only one way I could be stronger than him.

"Our Father, who art in Heaven, hollowed be thy name,"

"Stop that shit," he groaned, coming towards me slowly. I scooted back, trying to stay away, and kept praying.

"Thy Kingdom come, thy will be done, on Earth-" He snatched me up off the floor and pulled me to the kitchen where he grabbed a knife. My eyes widened. "Please, Derrick," I begged. I desperately wanted to see my son and G-mama again, and I was just startin' to try to have a relationship with my father.

"My name is *ANTHONY!*" I squeezed my eyes shut. I didn't wanna see the knife. I didn't wanna see the end coming, even though I knew. Shit had come full circle. "You doin' all that prayin,'" he mocked, breathing hard into my ear. He had his arms wrapped around me so tight it was hard to breath. "I followed you for months, got to know you, yo' family, yo' friends. Tried to get in where I fit in, ya know." I didn't wanna hear his reasoning. It didn't even really matter at that point. "It's a shame, the pussy is really good, even though I had to slip you a lil' somethin' to get it." I looked at him confused. "Yea, you kept them damn legs tight as hell. The head is better though." I was disgusted with myself and I felt so stupid. I hadn't been with anybody but

Terrell before him, and I had let this crazy bastard get in my head. "That ten thousand dollars was good, but I'm mad as hell I didn't get more than that outta you." So many things were going through my mind. Everything was jumbled, mistakes I had made, people I'd miss, what ifs... "You wanna know the best part though, the very best part?" I kept my mouth shut. I really didn't care, but I was sure he was gonna tell me anyway. I could hear his breathing getting heavier, like he was getting excited. He laughed a little. "The very best part," he paused to lick my ear. As bad as I wanted to cringe, I was careful not to move an inch. That knife was much too close to me. "was killin' that lil' punk ass baby daddy of yours." My knees buckled. Had I heard him right?! My heart broke. I felt nauseous, like I was about to lose all of my insides at any moment. I opened my mouth, not even knowing what I was about to say, but he kneed me in my back and I went down to the floor. He grabbed me, looked me dead in my face, and kissed me, smashing his lips onto mine. I tried to squirm away from him, but I couldn't move. When he did finally back up, I screamed. I gave it everything in me. He smiled at me, amused, then plunged the knife into my chest, silencing me.

1

"Isaiah, you goin' the wrong way. You makin' her look crazy!"

"She look fine, Mesha, dang, let me do this." I heard their voices before I saw them. I recognized Isaiah's scent immediately, and my heart warmed at the thought of him. I could feel the soothing bristles of a brush going across the top of my head.

"Naw move! You got my girl in here lookin' like a fool." For a quick second, I wondered what was going on. Then it hit me like a semi-truck, the same nightmare that had been playing over and over in my mind for what felt like forever. As hard as I tried, I couldn't piece together anything after I was stabbed. Somehow somebody had found me and got me to the hospital before he killed me. I felt my heart start to race at the thought of *him*. I clenched my fists and mustered up every ounce of strength in me. It was a struggle to peel my eyes open. With only a squint, the ceiling lights made it feel like I was going into shock. They were way too damn bright.

"She's waking up again." I heard Isaiah whisper. *Again*? It sounded like he didn't believe the words as he said them. How long had I been out?

"What?" Mesha's voice boomed from my other side. "Are you serious!?" I couldn't bring myself to move anything but my eyes. My vision was blurry and I had to strain to focus. All I could make out was blindingly bright, white light. I tried to speak, to at least say hi to them, but something was caught in my throat. I tried to reach up, but I couldn't move my arms. Tears started running down into my ears and I was getting extremely frustrated. *Why the hell couldn't I talk or fuckin' move?!* I built up all my irritation and started jerking whatever I could. It hurt like hell, even though I was barely moving.

"Go get the doctor!" Isaiah yelled. I heard Mesha curse before she ran out.

"JaLea," I heard my dad's voice on the side of me where Mesha had been. He rubbed my forehead, and when I finally focused on his face, I calmed down a little. "Welcome back, baby."

~~~

"So glad to see you up again, Ms. Washington!" A handsome, curly head doctor whirled into the hospital room grinning from ear to ear. *Again*? I tried to ask questions, but nothing was happening. "Hopefully you'll stick around for good this time." What was he talking about? And why the hell couldn't I speak? I figured once they got that tube out of my throat I'd be able to, but I still couldn't get any words out. A nurse rambled off numbers from the machines that were surrounding me, and the doctor looked through his folder of papers. I kept opening my mouth, but nothing was coming out! Something was definitely wrong. I looked over at Isaiah, Mesha and Aaron, pleading with them to help me. Somebody needed to explain things to me, and soon! They all looked at me with puppy dog eyes, like I was beyond pitiful. I *hated* that. I tried to reach up and grab my throat, but my arm was so heavy I couldn't lift it more than what had to be a couple of inches. I was getting irritated again. The doctor could sense my panic, and put his hand over mine. "We need you to try and stay calm." He rubbed my hand and spoke so softly that my heart rate started to drop back down. I looked at him, begging him with my eyes. *What is going on*?? He let go of my hand and Isaiah grabbed it. "I'm Dr. Ashwin." His mocha brown eyes were so warm that I immediately felt like I was in good hands. He was so personable and confident and professional. "I've been in charge of your care since you arrived, and I'm happy to say that it looks like you're progressing wonderfully."

"Yea because when we found you, Boo, yo' shit was-"

"*Mesha!*" Aaron cut her off. I tried to laugh, but all that came out was breath. My friend was never one to use a filter, or much common sense. I tripped off what she said then. 'When we found you...' I assumed she was talking about her and Isaiah. But where had they found me? How bad was I? Where was Derrick- Anthony...

whatever the hell his name was? Did they know it was him that did this to me?! "We're sorry, Dr. Ashwin," Aaron apologized. "Please go on."

"As I was saying," the doctor cleared his throat and continued. "You've been in a coma for the past 42 days..." *42 days*?! There was no way! He had to be lying! I looked at Isaiah and he nodded his head.

"You woke up a few times though," Isaiah said, I guess for reassurance. It didn't work. I started to get angry all over again.

"Yes, JaLea," Dr. Ashwin began again. "This is the third time you've woken up. The last two times you were up less than an hour, then slipped back into your coma. This time, however, it looks to be much more promising." He had the biggest grin on his face, but all I could think about was the 42 days I was away from my family. I remembered buying gifts and finally getting up the nerve to decorate for my baby for Christmas, and that same nigga had ruined it for us again! Just like he had when he killed Terrell. I closed my eyes, remembering his words. I gagged at the guilt of being with the man who stole my son's father from him. I had missed *42 days* with Lil Rell. There was no telling what he was thinking. He probably thought I had abandoned him. My eyes welled up with tears thinking about the pain my son must have been going through. I prayed they had had sense enough not to bring him to see me in a coma. I could only imagine what I was lookin' like. "Being that you were comatose for so long, we're going to have to monitor you closely to see what type of rehabilitation you need to undergo. Your body should feel weak, as

well as your voice. You haven't moved, spoken, or eaten on your own in over a month so I want you to take it very slowly, yes?" He nodded, prompting me to do the same, letting him know I understood. I didn't *like* it, but I understood. I couldn't help but wonder if I'd be able to talk again. Lord *PLEASE* let me talk again!! I thought about my G-mama. I hadn't heard her voice in years. I wondered if anybody had told her why I hadn't visited her. Would she even be able to process what was being said to her?
"I know this may be a bit much, but I've already disclosed the details of your injuries to your approved visitors. Do you wish to know right now?" I looked over at my family and they were all just staring at me, waiting for my answer. I figured it was as good a time as any. I looked at Dr. Ashwin and nodded at him again, ready to hear what that asshole did to me. He flipped through papers before he began. "Late December of last year, you were brought in unconscious and visibly battered. You had suffered 3 broken ribs, head trauma, and a fractured orbital socket. There was a significant stab wound to your chest which resulted in a punctured lung, and there was evidence of sexual assault." I felt Isaiah's grip on my hand get a little tighter, and I closed my eyes trying not to cry. That sick-*fuck*! I was gonna kill him! There was no other way around it. He had to die. He would not get the best of JaLea Michelle Washington. I was gonna walk out of that hospital and get back at his conniving ass if it was the last thing I ever did. I opened my eyes again and all I could see was red. "I know it's all very horrible and I am truly sorry for your pain." He seemed genuine, and I believed

that he was. "We fixed the broken ribs and the fractured right eye socket. We've been monitoring your brain waves and we're happy with the activity that we've seen. We repaired your punctured lung, and we also ran a battery of tests, just to make sure that there was no pregnancy or transmission of any diseases." I cringed. I'm not sure if the doctor was under the impression that I didn't know who my attacker was, but I knew damn well, and if he had something, then my stupid ass had already caught it. "You made it through your surgeries with no incidents, and thankfully, all of your tests came back negative. We were just waiting for your mind to tell your body to come back to us. It's seeming like this third time is a charm. The last two times you woke up, you still weren't responding, and eventually, slipped back into your coma." I said a quick prayer, begging God to let me stay awake. I needed to be around my people, see my son and my G-mama, value Isaiah's friendship more and keep making amends with Aaron. I'll be damned if I was gon' be laid up in the hospital for another *42 days*! Derrick... Anthony... whoever the hell he was, had gotten over on me, but I would *not* let him win! That nigga was gon' get his. That was a promise!

2

After the doctor left, Isaiah and Mesha followed, promising to come back later. Aaron went around the room, reading all the cards that had piled up over the past few weeks. I smiled while he read. There were so many of them from family, coworkers, and even friends of friends that wanted me to know they were praying for me.

"Me, Isaiah and Mesha were the only ones who were supposed to know where you were so people just started giving us stuff once they heard." Heard what? Was I in the news? Were they lookin' for Derrick?! Damnit I wanted to talk! I was gettin' pissed off! I focused on my voice and concentrated like I was straight doin' magic. I strained so hard I thought I was about to shit on myself. It paid off though.

"Wha-what..." Aaron almost fell flat on the floor trying to get to my bed.

"What was that, JaLea?" My throat was dry as hell, but I tried again.

"What..."

"Go ahead." I almost laughed. Aaron was so excited. For me, it was bittersweet. I finally heard my voice, but I sounded like a man. An old, alcoholic that had been smoking since he was a teenager.

"Happened?" I finally got the words out. Aaron teared up. He almost made me cry.

"What happened?" he asked and I nodded. "Baby, I'm gonna have to let Mesha and Isaiah tell you how they found you because I wasn't there. I didn't even want them to tell me all the details. Anything before that, I'm sorry, sweetie, you gon' have to fill that in on your own." I closed my eyes. I was right. Isaiah and Mesha found me... That couldn't have been easy. The way the doctor described everything, I know I would've lost it seeing either of them like that.

"Mirror?" I whispered. I tried to judge Aaron's face when I asked. He looked worried and I tried not to panic thinking about what I looked like. It had been 42 days. Had he beat me to the point where my shit couldn't heal or something?! How bad did I look?!

"The only mirror is in the bathroom. I don't know if I should move you or-" I immediately started nodding my head. That was the best thing he could've said. I know the doctor wanted me to take it slow, but now that I was awake, that bed was irking me. Even though Aaron looked uneasy and I knew he didn't wanna do it, he left and came back with a wheelchair. I offered very little help while he unhooked me from a couple of machines and eased me out of the bed. I was on my feet for only a few seconds, but it felt like forever. It seemed like I was carrying an extra 75 pounds, but my arms and legs looked like I needed some fried chicken and macaroni and cheese.

Aaron rolled me clumsily into the bathroom, trying not to roll over cords as he went. He flicked on the bathroom light and I stared at my reflection in disbelief. I still looked like myself, but my eyes were dark and sunken in and my face looked gaunt. I took a good look at my arms and legs and was surprised that, as heavy as they felt, they looked like sticks. I tried not to bust out crying. I didn't wanna look down my gown, but I was sure I didn't have any titties. I didn't even wanna think about my ass. I felt petty as hell, wondering when I'd be back to my normal thickness. Of all the things I had to be thankful for, primarily my *life*, being thick again was what I was trippin' off of at that moment.

"Everybody's here," Isaiah popped his head in the bathroom. I looked at him through the mirror, wondering what he thought when he saw me. I was a shell of what I had once looked like. He smiled at me with the same smile I had missed for months, like his feelings hadn't skipped a beat. I knew mines hadn't. I had to turn away though. I didn't feel at all like the same woman he had loved. I couldn't see how he could even see me the same.

"They are?" Aaron asked. I hadn't even really paid attention to what Isaiah had said.

"Who?" What I wanted to ask was 'who's here'? But 'who' was all that I could muster up. The couple of words I had spoken had burned passing my throat. Even though I was overly thankful that I even woke up from my coma, I was bombarded with negative thoughts of revenge and ungratefulness. I wanted my voice back. I wanted to take care of myself instead of being pushed around by my dad. I wanted my big titties and ass and thick hips back. What I wanted more than anything else though, was to walk out of that hospital and return the favor that Derrick so graciously gave. To see him laid up with his ass beat, to see him bloody with a fucked-up face, knowin' that he'd barely be able to see whoever was out there that gave a damn about him.

"You talked!" Isaiah scared the crap outta me. The happiness on his face made me smile.
"Well, we weren't supposed to say anything," Aaron grinned, "But when you woke up, we couldn't help but tell everybody!" I groaned. What the hell would make them think I wanted to see all those people in my condition? He must've seen the attitude in my face. "We didn't know they'd start showing up, so if you aren't up to it just let me know and we can send 'em home." He had to make me feel bad, right? People had been worried about me. Don't get me wrong, I wanted to see them too. I just didn't want them to see me. They say you're your own biggest critic, but I didn't wanna think about how they would react to what I looked like. Aaron and Isaiah staring at me didn't help the situation at all. I felt pressured into an answer, so I nodded, reluctantly.

Isaiah threw a blanket over my legs and another

one around my shoulders. I'm sure he was just being sweet, but my self-conscience was telling me he couldn't bare looking at my bird arms and legs. They were disgusting. That tube feeding shit had my body beggin' for some meat and potatoes.

When they wheeled me into the intensive care waiting room, I was so overwhelmed by the sea of smiling faces that I broke down into tears. They rallied around me, and I was warmed by the chorus of kind words, hugs and kisses. Isaiah pulled the blanket up from my shoulders and wiped my tears away.

"Mommy!" My eyes flew open. Isaiah's mom was standing in front of me with Lil Rell and he was trying his hardest to get out of her arms. The only reason I didn't jump out of that chair was that I physically couldn't. Kim put my baby down and he ran to me. When he hugged me, nothing and nobody else mattered. Those little arms made all the pain and thoughts of revenge fly out the window. I don't know if it was my sheer need to hold him or what, but I was able to get both arms around my baby. It seemed like he had grown so much in those few weeks. I wanted to go home right then and there, and pick up during the holidays where we had left off. But I had long ago learned that time was something you most certainly couldn't get back.

"You... sleep?" Rell's little voice asked. I could only smile and nod at him. He wasn't even two yet, and he had already lost his father and almost lost his mother. Just like that, my mind turned to revenge again.

3

Dr. Ashwin was *pissed*! He tried to stay calm when he caught me out of bed, but once he saw that the gang of people in the waiting room were there for me, he shut shit *down*! Not only was I supposed to be resting and taking it easy, nobody was even supposed to know where I was. Since I had come in all jacked up, no information was supposed to be given out about me at all. The way the doctor looked at me made me feel like a kid caught throwin' a house party. I thought I was about to get a whoopin'!

    I enjoyed the lil' twenty minutes I got to spend with everybody. I wasn't trying to talk much, I did more nodding and smiling. I think it helped me pay more attention to things that were goin' on around me. Kim and Aaron were doting on Lil Rell like they were his parents. I tripped off how close they were sitting, how they looked at each other, how they interacted. There was somethin' goin' on between them. Had to be. They had never been that friendly before and I didn't know whether to laugh or throw up. The two of them together was somethin' I didn't wanna have to get used to.

    I wasn't surprised at all that Theresa wasn't there. Our issues were almost too deep to overcome, but Mr. Charles and Erica seemed genuinely happy to see me up. I put on the same face that I had with everybody else, even though I couldn't stand seeing Erica pregnant. Just knowing that she and Isaiah were having a baby was enough. I didn't need to see it. And did she really have to go and get all cute and shit to come to the hospital? When I started paying more attention though, I noticed that she and Isaiah didn't say two words to each other. In fact, they seemed to be avoiding each other all together. I'd make it my business to find out what that was about. I couldn't help but tell myself that if Erica and Dr. Charles knew the truth about Derrick then they wouldn't have been at the hospital. Mr. Charles probably would've tried to explain away Theresa's role, even though she was being used by the enemy just like I was. No doubt he'd try and protect her at the same time he tried to throw me under the bus. I shuddered at the thought of what would happen if anybody ever found out that I had been messin' around wit' the bastard that killed Terrell, or that he had conned me into convincing Mr. Charles to fork over ten thousand dollars for some bogus scholarships. God only knew where that money was, or where Derrick was, for that matter. If he had been caught, somebody woulda said somethin' to me by now.

    I smiled at all my visitors and accepted the hugs and kisses as they left. Isaiah, Mesha, and Aaron stood around me like my protection. I tried to keep a straight face as Erica came up. I coulda sworn I caught a mean mug on her face as she looked behind me to where Isaiah was. I wanted to turn around and see his reaction so bad, but my neck felt like a twig trying to hold up a bowling ball. She gave me fake hug, then Kim brought Lil Rell to me and sat him in my lap again. I despised having to say goodbye to him. I wanted to beg Dr. Ashwin to let him stay, but I already knew the answer. I hugged my baby, trying my best to keep the tears away. He was such a strong, handsome lil' boy. Those curls and dimples reminded me so much of his daddy, I wanted to scream. For a quick second, I wondered how I could've stopped Derrick from killing Terrell. It hit me then, that I couldn't have. It was inevitable. Derrick had been out for blood for way too long.

    "Okay, sweetie. We're about to get up outta here," Aaron said, snapping me back to the present. I took one more long look at Lil Rell, kissed him on his forehead, and let him go so Kim could pick him up.

    "Bye, JaLea. It's so good to see those eyes again." Kim kissed me on my forehead and she and Aaron left. I smiled inside. *Uh-huh*. They *would* be leavin' together.

    "So look," Mesha popped her gum walking beside me as Isaiah wheeled me back to my room. "I'mma need you to not scare me like that again." I looked up at her and smiled. "No bullshit." She stopped the wheelchair dead in the middle of the hallway and stooped down in front of me. "You ridin', *I'm* ridin', heffa. I don't know what I'd do if I lost my best friend." She had tears in her eyes and I held my hands up for a hug. When she stood back up she was wiping her eyes. "Got a G out here cryin' and shit." I shook my head at her. "Ok, I'mma get on outta here." She stalled a little bit, gave Isaiah a weird look, and patted his shoulder. Again, I was dying to see his facial expression. What the hell was all the secrecy about?

"Alright, Mesha," Isaiah said to her. She kissed me on my forehead and left us walking back to my room in silence. He picked me up with little effort and settled me back into bed. He rubbed my head and stared at me with those hazel green eyes I loved so much. I almost felt uncomfortable but, for the life of me, I couldn't turn away.

"Erica?" It was the first thing that came to mind. He grinned at me and pulled a chair up.

"You don't waste no time, huh?" I cocked my head at him. I was serious as hell. "Let's not talk about her right now." The only thing that was keepin' me from bein' mad at that moment was his hand on my head. I wanted to know what was goin' on between him and his baby mama. Ugh... the words even sounded nasty in my head.

"What-- happened?" My throat was slowly but surely feelin' better, if you could call less burning 'better'. I was proud of myself, but Isaiah had a strained look on his face. I knew he didn't wanna relive it, but I needed to know. He rubbed his face and stared out into space.

"Mesha called me panicking. She told me... he was behind everything. The break-ins, the busted windows." He wouldn't look at me, but I watched, intently, as his jaw clenched. "She said you wouldn't answer her calls and you were on your way to his house- by *yourself*!" He looked at me then, and I shrunk back. I knew the questions that he had. Why did I go? Why didn't I call him? Why didn't I at least pick Mesha up? I knew he wouldn't ask me though, at least not right then. I had all the answers, even though laying up the hospital made them all seem stupid. I wanted to know why Derrick did what he did, what his problem was with me. It didn't dawn on me that he had to have a serious vendetta if he had gone to the extreme that he had. I didn't call Isaiah because I was convinced I'd lost him for good. And I didn't pick up Mesha because I wanted to get to Derrick as fast as I could so I could curse him out. It wasn't registering that he would do whatever he could to hurt me. I was on ten and wanted to get at his ass as soon as possible. "I went and picked her up so we could try and find you. It wasn't easy. All Mesha knew was that he stayed somewhere off Kingshighway and Chippewa. We drove up and down street after street, knocking on door after door, showing your picture, askin' people if they had seen you. After like an hour, we ended up on Lindenwood." I shuddered at the mere mention of the street. It gave me flashbacks that I didn't want or need. "We found an older woman who said she saw you visit her upstairs neighbor sometimes and she was pretty sure y'all had been arguing earlier." My heart was beating outta my chest. It felt like I was listening to a suspense story about somebody else. He looked down at the floor and took a deep breath before he continued. My eyes were big as hell, watching his every move. He was pissed and hurt and that jaw muscle was about to bust. "We kept bangin' on his door yellin' his name, until Mesha stomped off back to the car. We were scared and gettin' frustrated because you hadn't called anybody and we knew you wouldn't go anywhere wit' him. We had to believe we could find you." He looked back up at me with tears in his eyes. "And we did." We locked eyes and that's when I felt the tears. I didn't know they were coming, but I welcomed them. "We started riding down alleys, callin' your name, tryin' not to think the worst. He took you two blocks away... and left you behind a trash can." That sounded eerily familiar. He left me in an alley like my mama had done his brother. No surprise there. I'd expect nothin' less of him. I bet he didn't expect my people to find me though. "You looked... broken." His voice was weak. "There was so much blood. Mesha kept screaming. I was scared to touch you, or even lean in and make sure you were breathing." His voice was shaking and he kept wringing his hands. The lump in my throat hurt like hell. I wanted to scream to the top of my lungs. I wanted to cry for hours. I wanted to wrap my arms around Isaiah and assure him that I was gonna be ok. I slipped my hand behind his head and rested it on his neck. He grabbed my wrist and smiled. "I been up here every day, Lea, spending the night whenever I could, praying you'd come back to us. I know I was bein' a asshole, but I don't ever wanna think about losin' you again. These past few weeks been drivin' me crazy."

Tears streamed down his face and I cried right along with him.

~~~

The police had to have been keeping tabs on me, waiting for me to get my voice back. I hadn't been awake a good three days before they were hassling me. They had their jobs to do, and I guess I should've been thankful they were trying to solve my case. I was sure they hadn't gotten far, since they didn't have all the details.

"You sure you want me to leave?" Mesha asked. I nodded. She mugged the officers and I laughed. Typical Mesha. I needed her to leave though. I wasn't ready for everyone to know the whole truth. I waited for the detectives, Miles and Dixon, to introduce themselves, and I got straight down to business.

"Y'all are lookin' for the wrong person," I whispered. They automatically looked puzzled. "I know my friends told you his name was Derrick. That's what he told me at first, but his real name is Anthony Merritt. He's the brother of the man who killed my mama, and he killed my fiance'." It sounded like a Lifetime movie as it came out of my mouth, but I was dying to tell them the truth. They had to stop looking for 'Derrick'. I laid it all for them from beginning to end, trying to remember every single detail I could. It took every ounce of energy in me, but I had to do it. I told them everywhere we went, everything he said and did to me, any little memory I had of him, I told them. I didn't forget about Tasha and Theresa's asses either. They played their part too, and everybody had to get it. I wanted so bad to be the one to tell Theresa that she had been workin' with the man who killed her son. I wanna say that would be payback enough for me, but it would be a lie. I wouldn't be satisfied til' I saw every last one of 'em bleed.

4

"Good news, JaLea," Dr. Ashwin always twirled in my room like he had on skates. "It looks like we can send you home tomorrow." I almost got up out of the bed and hugged him before he even finished. I fought to keep myself calm while Isaiah and Aaron jumped and hugged in the corner like a couple of little girls. I was feeling a lot stronger, but I still didn't wanna pull or pop anything so I eased up and Dr. Ashwin came over for a hug.

"Thank you so much for everything. I don't think I can ever repay you-"

"Oh please, JaLea." He waved me off. "It's been my pleasure to help you through this journey." He hugged me again and when he backed up, he laughed. "If you really wanna repay me, convince Mesha I'm not available." I was cracking up. That girl was a complete mess.

I had come to love Dr. Ashwin and all my nurses, but I'd had just about enough of Barnes Hospital. I missed my baby. I missed my bed. As amazing as it was having breakfast, lunch, and dinner served to me, I missed being independent. I wanted to be able to rip and run and get out and have fun. I knew It wouldn't be easy. I'd still need help here and there, but I was more than ready.

While Aaron and Isaiah were getting all my things together, I couldn't help but think about what my first step would be. How would I get back at the people who hurt me? I wasn't sure Tasha would get anything more than a slap on the wrist, and I silently prayed I'd find Theresa and Derrick before the police did. It was cool to have them locked up, but that pain wouldn't be enough for them. I had rage in my heart so deep it almost scared me. I was tired of people fuckin' wit' me. I was at a point where I'd kill for anybody in my circle, small as it was. Lil Rell, G-mama, my mama, Mesha, and Isaiah. Kim knew her sister had it out for me and didn't say a word 'til it was about time for the shit to hit the fan. And I prayed Aaron had been steerin' clear of Theresa. Now the both of them were actin' all touchy, feely. Until I was sure of what the hell was goin' on, both of 'em were gettin' the side eye from me. There was no tellin' what kinda shit I was gonna get into when I got out, and whoever stuck wit' me, I knew I could count on them for the long haul. Whoever didn't, then fuck them too.

"Okay, JaLea, I think we got just about

everything." Aaron walked over with a box full of cards and I cocked my head at him.

"Wassup wit' you and Theresa?" After I asked him, I watched his reaction closely. He frowned up like I had farted or somethin'.

"Nothin' is up with me and Theresa. I saw her outside Schnucks a couple weeks ago and she ran." I took a good look at him, and he looked pretty good. He had a fresh cut, his lips weren't all dry and cracked like they used to be, his clothes were clean, he wasn't ashy, and it looked like he had picked up a little weight. His teeth were the only reminder that he had ever been on drugs. And even they didn't look as bad as I was used to 'em lookin'.

"Wassup wit' you and Kim?" I whispered, making sure Isaiah didn't hear me. He paused then, lookin' through that box of cards like he hadn't seen them before. "I know you heard me!"

"What?" he asked, like a lil' kid.

"Y'all doin' it?"

"JaLea!"

"What?! I need to know."

"No, we are not... doin' it, and you really didn't need to know."

"Yea, I really did." I smiled, even though I was disappointed. He was always a damn step ahead of me. First, he was wit' Theresa while I was wit' Terrell, now he was doin' whatever wit' Kim and I hadn't even had a chance wit' Isaiah. I rolled my eyes.

"It's nothin' serious, we just kinda got to know each other a little more while we were takin' care of

Rell."

"Mmm hmm." I left it alone right then, but he wasn't off the hook just yet.

~~~

I had to stop and see my G-mama. Aaron and Isaiah argued with me all the way there, telling me I needed to just go home and that it wouldn't really matter if I went right then, or a few days later. I wasn't budging. Whether she knew I was there or not, I was gonna see her. Aaron had told the staff I was in the hospital, but didn't elaborate on why. And I hated that I had to lie to my G-mama. I told her I was sick. I wanted so bad to believe that she could understand everything I was saying, but she stared straight through me like she had always done. I left feeling defeated. I could feel the 'I-told-you-so's' floating around as we rode to my house in silence. Neither Isaiah nor Aaron asked me how things went. They could see the disappointment on my face, so they just left me to my own thoughts, which I was thankful for.

My eyes lit up like it was Christmas when we finally pulled up to my apartment. The police had found my car a few blocks away from Derrick's apartment, and when they released it to Aaron, he and Isaiah cleaned it up for me in hopes that I'd wake up soon to drive it again. No telling when that would be, but it looked good sitting in front on the apartment. Isaiah helped me up the steps while Aaron carried my things. "Mommy!!" That little voice greeted me before we could even get to the door. I smiled from ear to ear at the sight of my son. That lil' boy was like magic to me. Mesha stood in the doorway with her arms crossed, smiling at us.

"I wish y'all would come on. You makin' everybody wait."

"Everybody? Like who?" She winked at me and shuffled me inside. The same smiling faces that had come to see me at the hospital had packed into my apartment to welcome me home! Kim and Mesha had purple balloons everywhere and I smelled chicken. It had been so long since I had some fried chicken, I was almost scared to eat it. I rejoiced in the music, fun, and Lil Rell. Being able to watch him run around meant everything to me. I decided at that moment that I would appreciate everybody and everything so much more. At any moment, it all could so easily be taken away.

I had been enjoying myself and my company, that is, until Mr. Charles caught me coming out of the bathroom. I thought he had just been waiting for me to get done so he could go, but he blocked me from going back into the living room.

"I know it was that lil' young punk you were laying up with who did this to you." For a quick second, I let myself believe that I heard sympathy in his voice. I was trippin'. "You conned me," he growled.

"Mr. Charles, I had no idea-"

"You always were as stupid as they come." He looked me up and down like I had shit all over me.

"Wait a minute Mr.-"

"You," he pointed his finger so close in my face, I smelled his tobacco. "You conned me out of thousands of my grandson's money."

"If anything, I was the one who was conned!" I

didn't know how he had gotten wind of who my attacker was, but it was just like him to make himself out to be a victim when I had been the one in a coma.

"You were just a stupid tramp who put your trust in that boy-"

"If I'm not mistaken, YOU gave your blessing-"

"I put my trust in someone I thought I knew and you blindly gave my grandson's money away."

"That's all it's ever about with y'all, money! Terrell and your parents, God rest all their souls, were the only level headed people in this family!"

"You're going to give me my money back-"

"Hey!" Aaron yelled and broke it up. "You can go ahead and leave now," he nodded at Mr. Charles and pointed towards the door. Mr. Charles glared at him, then at me, but I bet he stomped his behind out that door. I had half a mind to follow him and stick my foot in his ass. The confrontation had me sweatin' bullets, praying nobody got wind of who Derrick *really* was.

5

It took forever to get Lil Rell to sleep. That boy was on ten after all the excitement. I had to read him three stories before he finally drifted off. After I laid him down, I sat and watched as Mesha and Isaiah cleaned up for me.

"Don't nobody care you just got home, heffa! You can pick up a plate or somethin'!" Mesha joked. I flicked her off and looked over at Isaiah. I hated that just lookin' at him made my heart skip a beat. That man was so fine. He looked even better cleanin' my house. I could get used to that. Mesha clapped right next to my head and I damn near peed on myself.

"What's wrong wit'chu?!" I yelled at her. She nodded towards Isaiah and smiled.

"Feenin' ass," she whispered. I frowned and rolled my eyes. *Of course* she would catch me staring.

"What's wrong wit' y'all?" Isaiah walked over to the couch where we were.

"Nothin'," Mesha laughed. "Well, I'm about to be up, y'all." She hugged me and patted Isaiah on her shoulder. She gave him that same look she had given him in the hospital. I glared at her and got up to followed her out to the porch.

"So whats' goin' on?" I could barely wait to ask her.

"Whatchu mean?" she shrugged her shoulders and I squinted at her.

"You know what the hell I'm talkin' about. What's with all the lil' side eyes and funny looks between you and Isaiah?"

"You know I don't like tellin' people's business." I crossed my arms and cocked my head at her. "Ugh, I can't stand you!"

"I love you too," I told her. "Now wassup?"

"Man, all I'mma say is that me and Isaiah had a lot of long talks while you were in the hospital and he needs you just as much as you need him." I uncrossed my arms, letting my guard down. I felt like shit that, for a split second, I actually thought there was somethin' more there. I knew deep down that it couldn't be possible. "Say somethin'!" Mesha yelled.

"I don't know what to say."

"Heffa, you pulled the secret outta me and you don't even have nothin' to say about it?! I shoulda made you wait and let him tell you!"

"You didn't even tell me nothin' for real!" I was unable to stop smiling. She said Isaiah *needed* me.

"Bye, wainch." Mesha kissed me on the cheek and walked to her car. I stood on the porch watching her. How was I supposed to go back in the apartment and face him without cheesing like a high school girl? I swallowed my fear and walked back in to find him sitting on the couch. He was watching t.v. like he lived there. My chest started hurting thinking about the conversation we were hopefully about to have.

"You look comfortable," I told him, settling on the couch beside him.

"I am," he laughed.

"So, back to Erica." He started buggin' up! I was serious as hell. He looked at my face and cleared his throat, immediately calming down.

"Ok, back to Erica." He was silent for a minute. That was the most painful minute. I swear he wanted me to slap him! "It's not my baby, Lea." It felt like I'd been holding my breath for months, even before being in the hospital, waiting for him to say that. I forced myself not to break out smiling.

"How do you know?" I asked.

"She admitted that she was already pregnant when we hooked up. She's not due the middle of June. She's due the middle of May." He shook his head. "I had started spendin' most nights at the hospital and she was gettin' pissed-"

"How is she mad because you were visiting me at the hospital?"

"She saw somethin' we been tryin' to hide for

the longest." Oh shit. Here it comes. "Don't act like you don't know." He smiled that sexy ass smile and I had to look away.

"Isaiah," I looked down at my arms and the clothes that were basically hanging off me.

"You are still just as beautiful to me." He read my mind. "Even more so now. You are *strong*. You're a fighter and a survivor.

"I'm not." I shook my head and started to cry. He scooted closer to me and his scent filled my nostrils. He smelled so good that I had to close my eyes and take it in.

"JaLea, you are the most beautiful woman I have ever met. Your smile, your generosity, your sense of humor, your intelligence... all of that is so sexy to me. Watchin' you in the hospital, I realized there was no use fighting it anymore. I had tried to stay away from you and act like I didn't care, but this-" He stopped to rub my cheek and I opened my eyes. He was so close to my face, staring straight into my soul. I felt like I was melting. This man had the power to make me forget everything and everybody for the time being. It was just me and him on my couch and, at that moment, nothing else mattered. "I really can't see myself just bein' your friend anymore. I wanna be your protector. I wanna be your man, JaLea. I don't wanna sit on the sideline and watch you be lonely or watch you get hurt again." He was sayin' all the right things, makin' me feel all special. His eyes were makin' me melt. I felt like I was about to explode. "I been happy before, but I need you to make me feel complete." I couldn't think of how to respond. I couldn't believe what he was sayin' to me. He had never expressed himself like that. He'd flirt here and there. I knew he cared about me, but *damn*. He had laid his heart out and all I could do was *stare* at him. He smiled at me, showing those pretty, white teeth, and I smiled back. I couldn't help it. The moment seemed to move in slow motion as his hand slid around my back and he leaned in to me. I tried to ignore the fact that my heart was thumpin' outta my chest. I closed my eyes when our lips finally touched. At first, it was a peck, soft and gentle, then he sucked my bottom lip and I moaned and wrapped my arm around his neck. His tongue slipped into my mouth and he tasted so good. He held on to me and kissed me for an eternity. There was so much love and passion. When he pulled away, he looked at me and pushed my hair behind my ear. "I love you, JaLea." He didn't wait for a reply. Instead, he leaned back on the couch and pulled me onto his chest where we fell asleep.

~~~

The look on Kim's face when Isaiah told her we were together was priceless, and not in a good way. I always knew she looked at me like a daughter, and understandably so. My mama had been murdered, my G-mama had gone crazy, Tasha, who was supposed to be my mama's friend, was on my shit list for settin' her up. My dad had been strung out. I didn't have anybody else. Kim had stepped in and played the mother figure for me when I had lost every female in my life. She had done a damn good job too, but we weren't blood, no matter how much we acted like it. The love Kim had for me was that for family, but what I felt for Isaiah was nowhere near brotherly love. I knew Kim, and I knew she wanted the best for her son, as any mother should. She wanted Isaiah with a nice, wholesome, untainted business-orientated woman who'd treat him like a king and birth her five grandbabies. She wanted them to live happily ever after in a two-story, brick house with a white picket fence some damn where. That wasn't me. It was common knowledge that I was damaged goods. I accepted that, and so did Isaiah. I loved him with everything I had to offer. He understood me; my past, my pain, my hate, my demons; and he loved me regardless. He knew me like no one else ever would. I'd be damned if I let anybody else in my life just so they could stab me in the back...or in the damn chest.

"Well, that was-"

"A disaster," Isaiah finished my sentence. Lil Rell sat in the back giggling, oblivious to anything that was going on. I folded my arms and shook my head. I knew Kim wouldn't be over the top happy, but I hadn't expected her to question us so much. Why? Are you sure? What are your plans? Do you really have a future together? I wanted so bad to tell her to shut the hell up and get on board or get her ass left. She didn't come right out and say she didn't want us together, but she might as well have. I wanted so bad to bring up her and Aaron, but I wasn't exactly sure what was going on, and I didn't wanna start me and Isaiah's relationship off by arguing wit' his mama.

"I want you to know somethin'," I said, trying to change the sour mood we were both in. He nodded, but kept his eyes ahead. "You know Terrell didn't like you, right?" He burst out laughing.

"I'm not sure where you goin' wit' this, but ok."

"I just wanted to make sure you understand that I'll always love him for who he was to me, and even though he didn't like you, I wanna believe that he'd want me to be happy and with somebody who will love his son like their own."

"I understand that. You got me, baby." Isaiah reached around to rub my neck and I smiled. Yea, I got that ass, *finally*.

6

It was weird as hell to picture Derrick's face and think that his name was *Anthony* instead. I searched every memory I had of him, trying to find any tell-tale sign that he and the man that killed my mama were brothers. I wondered why I couldn't see it. Why I didn't catch it before it was too late? How the hell couldn't I have known?! Chris's eyes were burned into my memory from that night, and I didn't see it in Derrick at all until it was far too late. He played the shit outta me. And he did it so damn smooth, it was sickening.

There were countless nights that I parked outside his apartment waiting for any sight of him. I didn't have anything planned yet, I just wanted to see his face. It seemed like he had up and abandoned the place. I stalked corners where I knew Theresa used to be and never once caught a glimpse of her either. They both seemed to have vanished into thin air. Isaiah had spent weeks hounding the police to find them. I tried to be completely open with my feelings, without tellin' him I actually went on stake-outs. He knew I was seein' red, every day, all day. I wanted blood, and Isaiah didn't want me to run into Derrick or Theresa before the police did. He prayed with me, trying to help tame the fire that was growing inside. I had an itch, though. Unfortunately, the police weren't helping me scratch it.

~~~

"You lookin' good and healthy," Mesha said as we rode around. I needed some air, and she was more than happy to pick me up.

"Thank you, boo." I twirled my hair and smiled. She was right, though. I had been eatin' my ass off, partly because I felt like skin and bones bein' wheeled outta the hospital, but mostly because I missed food! "Isaiah been keepin' me full."

"Yea I bet he has," she commented.

"Anyway," I laughed, knowing full well we hadn't done anything yet.

"I'm so glad y'all finally stopped bein' retarded!"

"We got together when we needed to get together," I told her.

"Yea, ok wit' all that written in the stars crap." I shook my head at her. "Old it-was-meant-to-be-when-it-was-meant-to-be lookin' asses," she continued.

"Whatever." I rolled my eyes.

"So when we beatin' Erica ass?" My mouth flew open. "Heffa don't act like you don't wanna beat her ass!" I smiled, thinkin' about it. The thought had run through my mind plenty of times, even before she had claimed she was pregnant by Isaiah.

"Can we at least wait 'til after she has the baby?" I asked. Mesha sucked her teeth.

"I guess," she sneered as we pulled up to Page and Belt. "Well I'm ready when you ready," she said, tapping on the steering wheel. All of a sudden, her eyes got big. I followed her gaze and, sure enough, there was Theresa straggling around like the walkin' dead. I automatically started poppin' my knuckles, damn near gettin' wet thinkin' about poundin' her ass into the sidewalk. My phone rang, breaking my trance and I looked down to see Isaiah's face. Babe was gonna have to wait. "JaLea," Mesha warned. "We're in public-"
BEEEEEEP!!

The car behind us honked its horn, urging us to go. I snapped my head up at the green light and hopped out of the car before Mesha had a chance to put her foot on the gas. I heard her calling my name, but I was in my own zone. I hurried across the street and ran up on Theresa's dirty ass.

"Theresa." I called her name and gave her just enough time to register that it was me before I clocked her in her damn eye. She stumbled and the couple of fiends that were with her slithered off. The look on her face was hysterical. It was a mixture of fear, pain, and confusion. I lost it. I rushed her, knockin' her to the ground so I could drop down on top of her. I went to town on her face and her chest, not even feelin' bad that she wasn't fightin' back. Fuck her. The blood spilling from her face only excited me. I swung, uncontrollably, until I felt somebody pulling me away.

"Come on, boo. That's good enough, Lea." Mesha had my arms. I was able to give Theresa one good kick before Mesha dragged me away. Watching Theresa squirm on the ground made me want more.

"My bitch *CRAZY*!" Mesha yelled, speeding away from the corner.

"I don't know why you pulled me off her!" I yelled back.

"I was tryin' to keep you outta jail, heffa!"

"It felt so *good*, Mesha!"

"Yea, you look like it did! You didn't hold nothin' back! You woulda killed her ass if I hadn't pulled you off." I knew she was joking, but it scared me a little bit. If she hadn't been there, who woulda stopped me? When we pulled in front of my apartment, Mesha stared at me.

"What?!"

"You look a mess." I flipped the visor down and sure enough, my hair was all over my head. I straightened my clothes and pulled a brush out of Mesha's glove compartment to brush my hair back into a ponytail. "That's cool and all, but how you gone hide that?" Mesha pointed to my hands. I hadn't paid attention to how bloody and torn my knuckles were. With all the adrenaline running through me, I hadn't even felt any pain.

"Shit," I mumbled. My phone rang and it was Isaiah. "Hey, babe. I just pulled up, I'll be in in a minute."

"Ok, I was startin' to worry 'cause you weren't answering your phone."

"Good luck," Mesha joked. I walked in the house scared as hell. I had no idea what I was gonna say, but as soon as Isaiah stepped towards me, I shoved my hands in my pockets and leaned into him when he hugged me.

"Ok, wassup with that weak hug?" Isaiah held me at arms-length and looked me up and down. I didn't know what to say, so I just stared at him. "Did I do somethin'?" he asked, looking confused. When I still didn't answer, he dropped his hands from my arms and stood back. His expression went from confusion to anger. "Lea... did YOU do something?" I started stammering tryin' to explain myself. There was a big difference between tellin' him how bad I wanted to hurt somebody, and actually doing it. He put his hands back on my shoulders to calm me down. "Tell me what happened, baby." I had to look down at my feet while I talked to him. I had to hide the fact that I actually liked it. I wasn't stutterin' because I regretted what I did. I just didn't want Isaiah to be disappointed in me. When I finished, I pulled my hands out of my pockets to show him. He groaned and dragged me to the bathroom. He turned the water on and gently washed the blood from my hands. I winced and griped, but he stayed quiet until he finished cleaning and drying my hands. He sat me on the couch and looked at me. "I will go to war wit' any nigga that hurt you, but you can't go around beatin' people's ass like that in public, baby. You need to let yo' man handle things." I almost said *yes sir*! I looked at him and nodded. I'd let him have his way, I didn't know how long I could handle that though.

7

"Mommy, the door!" Lil Rell was runnin' his spoiled butt around the house. He made his way over to me and grabbed my hand to pull me to the door and I almost threw him out the window! My hands were killing me. I snatched away from him and had to apologize for hurting his feelings. Looking through the peep hole made me groan. It was Mr. Charles. Reluctantly, I opened the door. He stormed in and immediately started goin' off, sending Lil Rell running.

"And just who do you think you are? You can't go around putting your hands on people. You're lucky my daughter didn't call the police on you!" I giggled, thinking she probably couldn't remember the number wit' her crackhead ass. "You think this is funny? I've got half a mind to turn you in myself!" I rolled my eyes at him. He wasn't gonna call anybody. He got much too much excitement from bein' in my face blowin' smoke.

"What's goin' on?" Isaiah walked in and scooped Lil Rell up on his hip.

"He's mad I beat his daughter's ass."

"Oh my, why am I not surprised? I see you don't waste time, do you? Either of you," Mr. Charles commented, looking from me to Isaiah. "It's astounding how little time it took you to move Erica's guy into my grandson's apartment to take care of his baby." Out of the corner of my eye, I saw Isaiah put Lil Rell down and shoo him to the back.

"See now you old and you gettin' confused. This," I pointed to Isaiah. "This is not *Erica's* guy. This is *my* guy. And *this*," I made a circle around myself. "This is *my* apartment-"

"That you bought with my grandson's money!"

"Here we go again wit' the money! Let me hip you to somethin' and I want you to listen, and listen good. Terrell didn't just make sure his son was taken care of. He did the same for me. As much as you and Theresa wanna deny it, he loved me. I could be livin' lavish if I really wanted to but I'm not a lousy bitch. I do work, thank you very much. But even if I wasn't workin'. Even if I was out here rockin' a different pair of Louboutins for every day of the month. Even if I was drivin' around in a Maybach and livin' in a big stupid ass house in Baldwin, that would be *my* business, *not* yours. But guess what, ya girl is smarter than the average bear, ok. I know how to stack and save. We stay in a two-family flat in the Central West End. I kept my Charger and I still dress me and my baby because I want to and I *can*. So-"

"I guess he's gonna help you spend it since you wasted no time getting him in here." Mr. Charles frowned and nodded.

"Did you miss the point wit'cho stubborn ass? I spend my money the way JaLea wants to spend it. I'm far from stupid, boo. Truth be told, I trust him way more than I trust any of y'all Sanders."

"Funny you say that, judging by how bad you wanted to be one."

"Terrell wasn't like you and you daughter. He was like your parents, God rest all their souls. I can't for the life of me figure out how you and Theresa got to be so fucked up."

"You don't even respect your elders, talking to me the way you are."

"Oh I know very well how to show respect. I just don't like yo' ass."

"And I don't like your ass either." Mr. Charles moved towards me and Isaiah was between us in an instant.

"Look, I don't know what you think is about to go down," he told him, "but I suggest you suck it on up and take yo' feelings back on the other side of that door."

"Or *what*?" Mr. Charles tried to step up and I moved back to the couch to watch how things would play out. He wasn't the typical, frail old man. He was still nice and healthy for his age, but Isaiah had him by a few inches and at least thirty pounds.

"Look," Isaiah laughed a little, pissing Mr. Charles off. "I don't wanna have to hurt you, man."

"Look," Mr. Charles mocked, "If she puts her hands on my daughter again, I'll break her in half." That was all it took. Isaiah grabbed Mr. Charles and spun him around, twisting his arm behind his back.

"Are you crazy?!" he yelled out in pain.

"Not at all. I let my woman handle you for a minute so she could get her issue off, but you ain't gone come in this house and threaten her without dealin' wit' me. Now, like I said before, you need to get yo' old ass out." He shoved Mr. Charles, making him stumble a little towards the door. I giggled as he turned around and glared at us, straightening his jacket and his hat. I waited for him to say something, but he knew better. He turned and walked out, leavin' my door wide open wit' his petty ass. Isaiah went and stood in the doorway watching him leave, then slammed it shut. "Don't let his ass back in," he told me before he stormed to the back. I grinned to myself and looked out the window, congratulating Mr. Charles. I never did like him, but he had just made it to my hit list.

"Don't trip off him," I told Isaiah.

"I'm not trippin' off him." He walked past me and I grabbed his arm.

"You're not trippin' off what he said about livin' in Terrell's apartment?" He stared at me for a minute.

"Listen, just like you told him, I know you work. I also know Terrell left you money. I'm not threatened by it, ok? Stop tryin' to make an issue where there is none." With that, he turned and left me in the living room.

8

"*S*urprise!!" I almost peed on myself! In all my 25 years, I had never had a birthday party, let alone a surprise party. Isaiah and Mesha's sneaky butts had planned one for me. They got me good too. Mesha had picked up Lil Rell so Isaiah could take me to dinner, or so he said.

"Damn, baby, I left my wallet." He stood in the middle of my living room patting his jacket and pants pockets with an attitude. "I'mma have to stop at the house right quick." I didn't mind at all. I had been out of the hospital two months and I was just thankful to have lived to see another birthday. Lord knows I coulda been six feet under. Of course, when we pulled up to the house, he had an excuse to get me inside. "I gotta run to the bathroom, so come in and give me a minute." He ran in and I sat on the couch and waited. It wasn't long before he was rushing back out. "Let's go out the back so I can set this alarm for the front door." I frowned at him, thinking that we had never done that before, but I still wasn't expecting a gang of people to surprise me! I wanted to break down and cry, I was so touched.

Purple streamers and balloons decorated the back yard, hanging from the trees and on tables. There was food and people everywhere.

"We got you good," Mesha teased. I nodded as I was bombarded with hugs. I mingled and laughed for a while until Isaiah snatched me up.

"You havin' fun, birthday girl?" he asked me. Our moment was ruined before I could answer.

"Oh so that's what it is?!" I turned to see Erica standing behind me with her arms crossed. I rolled my eyes. Obviously, she felt some kinda way about seeing me and Isaiah together, plus, her lil' feelings were probably on ten since she was almost eight months pregnant. I wasn't tryin' to hear it either way, especially on my birthday.

Isaiah walked up on her and I had to strain my ears to hear him. "This ain't the time or place to have this discussion, Erica." He talked to her calmly, trying to keep things under control.

"No, we gone do this shit right here, right now." I crossed my arms and leaned against the nearest tree. Her ass was trippin', but I wanted to sit back and see how Isaiah was gon' handle her.   "I thought you just cared about her and wanted to help out while she was in the hospital. I didn't wanna believe my uncle when he told me, but *that's* the reason we ain't together." She flung her hand in my direction. The heffa had one more time to call me a 'that'. Isaiah moved in closer and growled.

"Oh you know damn well why we ain't together. Now if you want all yo' business out then we can do this." He was pissed and beyond disgusted. The look he gave her was like tellin' her she wasn't shit. She saw the same look that I did, and backed up a little. By that time, the party had stopped and everybody was staring in our direction. Erica looked uneasy, like she didn't know what to do next. When Isaiah turned and looked my way, Erica clicked and charged at me. I wasn't expecting it, and her lil' quick ass got the corner of my mouth real good. I had just enough time to clock her dead in her eye before Isaiah grabbed her and slung her away from me. I tasted blood on my lip and that pissed me all the way off, but the look on Erica's face was priceless. She had one hand over her eye in disbelief and I watched her face twist up while Isaiah wiped blood off my lip. "You good?" he asked me. I smiled and nodded, never taking my eyes off Erica. Petty... I know.

"What you waitin' for, bitch?! *Bye*!!" Mesha yelled walking up beside me. Erica rolled her eyes and turned to storm through the gang way. "Ugly ass," Mesha groaned. "Dang, all I did was go pee! What the hell I miss?!" I laughed and told Mesha what had happened as the rest of the party slowly got going again.

"I don't want you fightin' over me." Isaiah chimed in when I finished.

"Boy please, I don't have to fight over you, I already got you."

"Damn, well ok then," he laughed.

"*She* was tryin' to fight over you. I was defending myself. She'll be lucky if don't beat her ass after she have that baby, just for the hell of it."

"Girl don't waste yo' time on her jealous ass. It's yo' birthday!!" Mesha pulled me to the middle of the yard and started poppin'. I laughed at her and continued to try and enjoy myself, trying not to trip off of what other problems Erica would give me.

~~~

"So outside of the b.s. you really had a good time?" Isaiah had asked me that at least four times between his house and mine.

"Yes, baby," I laughed. "You think I'm lyin'?"

"You just been through so much bullshit. I really wanted today to be special for you. I'm sorry she had to come around messin' stuff up."

"I know, and I appreciate it. I had fun, ok?" I hadn't noticed that we had been moving closer and closer to the bedroom. Isaiah was trying to be slick. He had never pushed the issue before, but I can only imagine what the wait had been like. He'd hold me against him at night and I'd have to force my body to not react to him and to focus on healing. But it was my birthday. And he was makin' me weak, staring at me wit' those eyes. "I know what you're doin'," I told him.

"And what's that?" His voice was low. I knew what time it was. We had beat around the bush for years. He bent down and kissed me, like he had done hundreds of times before, but this one had some business behind it. He was ready for me and I was more than willing to give in. He picked me up and I wrapped my legs around his waist, letting him take me into the bedroom. We tore at each other's clothes, wasting no time getting naked. He bit his lip as his eyes roamed the length of my body. I was proud of the weight I had picked up. I was getting thick again in all the right places and almost back to my normal self. I stared at his tight body, his arms, his chest, that six pack, and that dick had my mouth watering. I had never seen him fully naked and he was *everything*! I exhaled, wondering if I could handle him. Hell, it had been *months*. Finally, he closed the space between us and started in on my neck. He knew that was my spot and he didn't let up. His hands were everywhere, makin' me feel like there were two of him. I threw my head back when his mouth moved down to my chest. I could hear him moaning as he worked his way down my stomach and spread my legs. He pushed me back on the bed and dove in. He kissed those lips the same as he kissed the ones on my face, makin' me squirm and grab the back of his head. I couldn't believe I had waited so long to give in to him. He had me goin' and hadn't even stuck it in yet. His tongue game was so strong, I had to beg him to stop. He licked back up the length of my body until his eyes were level with mine. The pressure between my legs damn near had me feeling like a virgin. I resisted the urge to scream out in pain, but he moved slow, kissing me and lookin' in my eyes. "You feel so good," he whispered. I couldn't even respond. He filled me all the way up, causing tears to build up and slide into my ears. He had a rhythm and I rocked with him, holdin' on for dear life. The initial pain had left and all I felt were shock waves with every move he made. He was gentle enough to not hurt me, but gave me enough power to let me know who was in charge. He stroked long and slow, then sped up, grunting and tellin' me how good it was. I bit into his arms and chest, yelling his name and scratching his back. I had seriously been missin' out. I don't know if it was just that I hadn't had any in so long, or that I had always wondered what he was workin' with and finally got some, or if he was just that damn good! Either way, I was addicted just that quick.

I woke up the next morning rejuvenated as hell and I could feel the grin on my lips before I even opened my eyes. The smell of bacon pulled me up out of bed. I wrapped a sheet around my naked body and strolled into the kitchen where Isaiah was cooking breakfast. I smiled at the fresh scratches on his back. Just the sight of his tight back and the thought of what was under those boxers had me lickin' my lips thinkin' about the work he put in the night before.

"Good morning," he said without turning around.

"How did you know I was even here?"

"With them heavy ass feet and hard breathin'?" I ran up to hit him on his arm and he turned around and grabbed me. Those damn green eyes! "I love you."

"I love you too." It felt so good to hear him say that and to say it back to him. I let him go back to the food and settled on the couch, watching him. Lord I wanted to be happy so bad. But I couldn't help thinking that something was bound to go wrong. Things couldn't possibly be that perfect.

9

"How many times we gotta sit outside this nigga apartment? His ass ain't comin' back here, Lea. I got a new piece of man meat and he been wantin' to see me. He is fine as shit, *and* he bow-legged. I bet he could knock a bitch walls clean out. Oooh weee, I'mma grab them damn curls on his head-"

"Mesha shut up!" I whispered. "You throwin' me off."

"Off what?! We sittin' in the dark at midnight starin' at a damn window like some stalkers." I rolled my eyes but didn't turn her way. "Ugh I can't believe I let you talk me into this shit again." She huffed and slouched in her seat like a kid. "You might need to see somebody for some help." I almost snapped my neck turnin' to look at her.

"I can guaran-damn-tee if you went through

what I went through you'd be doin' some off the wall shit too. You got me beat hands down in the crazy department."

"Forget you-" She stopped mid-sentence and her eyes got big. I turned back towards the apartment to see what made her react. There was a faint light in Derrick's window. My heart sped up so fast it felt like I was havin' a panic attack. I had to pace myself like I was breathin' through labor pains. There was that all too familiar phantom pain that hit my chest every time I was on his street. My palms were itchin' so bad. They wanted some action in the worst way. I couldn't believe out of all the nights I had parked out in front of his apartment, that the time had finally come. "Whatchu gon' do?" Mesha whispered. I slid on my gloves that I had stashed in the glove compartment and grabbed the bat I had in the back seat.

"What'chu think?" I flung the door open. "I'm 'bout to kill this bitch."

"*Lea*!" Mesha hissed after me as I slithered across the street. "Lea!" she called a little louder. I didn't stop until I was posted against the wall of the building. Nervousness and adrenaline had me sweatin' bullets by the time Mesha caught up wit' me.

"You stay here and call me if he decide to be brave and come out the front," I instructed her.

"Ok, Lea," she grabbed my shoulders. "Let's slow down and think rationally-"

"*Forty-two* days."

"What?" She let me go and cocked her head.

"Forty-two days he stole from me. Christmas

wit' my family, huggin' my son, kickin' it wit' my best friend. And even when I got out I had to take it easy. He *stabbed* me, beat the *shit* outta me, and *raped* me. I had broken ribs and a collapsed lung. I couldn't even talk when I woke up. I'm blessed to even be here because if he woulda had his way, I wouldn't be. He left me in the alley to die-" I stopped. Those were the same words Chris had said to my mama before he killed her. It was ironic as hell how somethin' that happened to my mama as a teenager had me in the situation I was in as a grown woman. I'm sure she never thought that defending herself would fall back on me. I didn't blame her at all. Life happens, and you gotta deal wit' it.

"Boo, I'm not tryin' to downplay anything that crazy asshole did to you." I hadn't noticed until just then that Mesha had tears in her eyes. "I just don't wanna see you get in trouble. What will happen to Lil Rell?"

"I haven't told anybody else this except for the police." I took a deep breath and closed my eyes. "Ok, so I told you about Chris, the dude who killed my mama?" Mesha rolled her eyes and nodded her head. "Derrick is his brother."

"Wait, what?"

"His real name is Anthony. And he stalked me for months, trying to get back at me for his brother goin' to jail. He conned me, got close to me, stole money from me, but on top of all that..." I stopped. I had to say it. I had started the conversation so I had to finally admit to somebody why Derrick had done the things he had done and how stupid I had been.

"What?" Mesha's mouth was hangin' open.

"He killed Terrell." It seemed like time stood still. Mesha just stared at me. All I could hear was her breathing. Then she grabbed me and squeezed me. She held me for what felt like forever.

"I'm so sorry. Oh my God, I'm so sorry," she kept repeating. "What if somebody sees you?" she whispered.

"That's what you're for, sis. Just yell if you see anybody coming." We backed away from each other and there was a look of understanding. I took off towards the back of the building, knowing Mesha wouldn't leave me. She was the definition of loyal, no matter what.

Fifteen minutes passed and I was getting antsy as hell. My phone vibrated, scarin' the shit outta me. I looked down and it was Isaiah. It was well after midnight but he was gonna have to wait. My phone vibrated again and it was a text from Mesha.

You think he went to sleep?

Hell naw he ain't sleepin' here, I thought to myself. No way. And I was right. The back screen door creaked open and slammed shut, making me snap my head up from my phone. There he was walkin' to his car wit' his fat ass. I gagged and tasted throw up in my mouth. I could feel his knife goin' into my chest, and had to count myself out of a panic attack. I thought of every day of my life that I had missed because of him, built up every ounce of anger I had in me, and walked up to him. I gripped the bat so hard my palms started to ache.

"Hey... *Derrick*." My voice came out in a whisper, and he froze. Even if he didn't recognize my voice, he knew his real name wasn't Derrick. I wasn't nervous anymore, I was tryin' not to get physically sick. The sight of him, even just lookin' at his back, made my stomach turn and chest ache. He turned slowly, and I gave him just enough time to get a glimpse of me before I swung the bat, catching him in the ear. He yelled and flew back against the car, grabbing the side of his face. I swung again, this time I got his dick. He doubled over and I hit him in the back. He yelled out and all that did was excite me. I felt empowered, swingin' over and over again, never giving him a chance to recover. I landed one last blow to his face before somebody grabbed me, making me drop the bat. Instantly, I got pissed because Mesha's ass was supposed to be watchin' out for me, but it was her. She pulled me to the opposite side of the building.

"It's people comin'," she blurted out. She was so outta breath that I almost didn't understand her. I stopped right before we got to the street, pulled my gloves off and came up outta my hoody and jogging pants, turning them inside out. "What the fuck you doin'?" Mesha asked me, staring in disbelief at the second layer of clothes I had on.

"Act normal," I told her as I walked calmly across the street. She scurried behind me and watched as I put my bloody clothes in a plastic bag and climbed in the car. "You comin'?" I called to her. She hopped in and I pulled off before she could get the door closed good. We rode in silence for a couple minutes. I could feel her staring a hole in the side of my face. "*What*?!"

"You know I'mma ride wit' you, but this ain't beatin' Theresa wit' yo' fist. That was actually kinda funny. But damn Lea, when I came around the corner and saw how you were swingin' that bat like a crazy woman-"

"Maybe I am a lil' crazy. You never went through the shit I been through so you don't know. You scared and trippin', but I feel *rejuvenated*. I feel so good I can't even put it in words."

"What if somebody saw us? What if you get caught?"

"Calm down, Mesha. I found the bat in a park and put it in a bag. I never touched it wit' my bare hands. I'm pretty sure it's blood on those clothes, but they're rolled up in a bag and I'mma dump 'em before I go home. When Derrick can talk again, he ain't gone run his mouth because he'd have to admit why he got his ass beat in the first place." I had to force myself to keep the smile off my face. Mesha was already spooked enough. "I been checked to make sure ain't no cameras outside the apartment, and I wore gloves. We good." I tried my best to reassure her.

"Oh, so you the perfect criminal now, huh?" Out of the corner of my eye, I saw her fold her arms and relax a little.

"Naw boo, I'm not a criminal. I'm just a chick on a mission who watch way too much First 48."

10

I had to drop Mesha off, then find a few different alleys to dump the gloves, and clothes I had on. It was after two by the time I crept into the house. I eased the door shut, being careful not to wake Isaiah or Lil Rell. I tried to sneak through the living room, tiptoeing as softly as I could. I let out a quick yell when the lamp clicked on. I stopped short of the entrance to the hall as Isaiah rose from the couch and cut me off. He towered over me in only his sleeping pants. I tried not to pay attention his rock-hard chest, beautiful abs, and that damn 'V' leading down to his-

"JaLea!" The sound of his voice made me jump to meet his eyes. Those things had turned dark like mood rings changing colors. He looked so upset, I had to back up a little bit. I could see all the anger and disappointment in his eyes and I almost felt ashamed.

"Zay-"

"Shut up!" he yelled. *Yes sir*, damn! "I'm tired of you treatin' me like a baby sitter while you slide outta bed every time I spend the night. If I didn't know what you were doin', I'd swear you was out there fuckin' somebody!"

"Zay-"

"Naw, I ain't tryin' to hear *nothin'*! I called you twelve times! I didn't even count the text messages! The *only* reason I didn't leave here lookin' for you is because of Lil Rell. I wanna kill these muthafuckas too, believe that, but you got a son to think about. What's gon' happen if you leave up outta here and don't come back?" He made me feel small as hell. Mesha had said the same thing, but it was different when Isaiah said it. The way he looked at me made me feel stupid.

"I'm sorry, Isaiah. I never meant to make you feel like a baby sitter. It's just that every day he's free I get more and more pissed off. I can't get it outta my head-" Isaiah turned before I could finish my sentence, and left me standing alone in the middle of the living room.

~~~

"Mommy! Door!" Lil Rell yelled.

"Okay, baby." I walked right past Isaiah on my way to the door. He'd had a nasty ass attitude wit' me for the past two days. He wasn't the only one who could act stank. I glared at him all the way to the door, but his stubborn ass never looked up from his magazine. I looked out the peep hole and saw Miles and Dixon, the two detectives that come to question me in the hospital. I panicked for a quick two seconds, then put my game face on and opened the door.

"Good morning, Ms. Washington," they greeted me in unison.

"Good morning, detectives." I smiled at them, making sure I wasn't grinning too hard. I didn't wanna give it away that I knew something was goin' on. "Y'all got news about my case?"

"Can we come in ma'am?" Dixon, the fat one, asked. I moved over to let them in.

"Detectives." Isaiah held his hand out and they all shook. I was gettin' irritated. I wished they would just question me and move the hell on. They were handin' out hellos and smiling all nice. I knew this wasn't a friendly damn visit. And I knew what I had done. They weren't there to arrest me. I was positive they had nothing, except for a strong motive, and that wasn't shit without any evidence.

"We do have some news about your case, Ms. Washington." Isaiah stood beside me and put his arm around my shoulders. I knew he was trying to be protective and be there for me, but I was a big girl and I could handle those two bum ass detectives, no problem. "Early this morning, we took an Anthony Merrit a.k.a. Derrick Meyer into custody."

"What?" Isaiah snatched his hand off my shoulder and glared at the detectives. I had been toying with the idea of telling him the whole truth. I had made him think things were the other way around, with Theresa and Tasha recruiting Derrick to follow me. He didn't know Derrick was the mastermind, or that his name wasn't even Derrick, or who he really was. Why I hadn't felt comfortable enough to tell him what was really goin' on was beyond me. It wasn't the time though. The truth would have to wait.

"Okay," I smiled, "You have him in custody. What's the next step. What do I need to do?"

"Well," one of the detectives started, "We found him under suspicious circumstances." I tried to look as confused as I could.

"He's in custody, but he's been brutally assaulted," the other one chimed in. We all looked back and forth at each other quietly for a few seconds. I knew they were waitin' to see what my reaction was.

"Well karma is a bitch, ain't she?" I smiled. The glared at each other, and Isaiah was staring a hole into the side of my face. "What?!" I yelled. "Y'all expect me to be sad somebody beat his ass? Hell naw! Y'all saw first-hand what he did to me. Y'all were there! So *oh well*." I crossed my arms, waiting.

"Where were you between midnight and 1 a.m., Tuesday morning?" I let off a little laugh.

"I was here. Asleep. With my man and my baby." They instinctively turned to Isaiah, who cocked his head at them.

"She was here," he answered.

"All night?"

"*All night*," Isaiah answered, this time with an attitude.

"She couldn't have slipped out while you were asleep?"

"I'm a light sleeper."

"Well okay, we just have to cover all our bases." The detectives stared from me to Isaiah. "I guess we'll be going then."

"Wait a minute! So what's gonna happen now? Will he be charged?"

"Right now, it's an ongoing investigation-"

"Ongoing investigation?!" I snapped. "How is that? I told you who it was, I even gave you his alias. I can pick him out of a lineup if you need me to. What else do you want?"

"Like I said ma'am," Detective Miles was talking to me like I was slow and it was making my blood boil. "We have an ongoing investigation, and we'll update you with details as we can. Right now, the victim can barely speak."

"*Victim*?!" I couldn't believe what I was hearing. Isaiah immediately stepped past me and opened the front door to let them out.

"If you could keep us updated, detectives, we'd surely appreciate it," he told them. Once they had pulled off, Isaiah slammed the door so hard a picture fell off the wall. He spun around fast as hell, huffin' and turnin' red and shit. I just knew he was about to swing. "You really tryin' me, Lea." He whispered so low, I almost didn't hear him. I walked up to him to try and explain myself. "What- did- you- do?!" I jumped clean back by the kitchen. He followed me, forcing me towards the hallway. "Tell me what you did, JaLea!" His voice boomed.

"Mommy?" Lil Rell called. I turned and he was right at my heels.

"Go back in your room, baby. Mommy and Mr. Isaiah are talking ok." He smiled and turned to run back down the hall. To be so young and naive again... I didn't wanna turn back around and face Isaiah, but I had to. I was trying to ready myself. I had never seen him so mad. I didn't know whether to talk or run.

"I swear, JaLea, if you don't start talkin' right damn now-"

"I caught him behind his apartment and beat him wit' a bat." There. I said it, but his facial expression didn't change at all. I leaned against the wall and just waited to see what he was gon' say. This nigga started laughing! I stared at him in disbelief until he stopped a few seconds later.

"Ugh," Isaiah groaned. "And when he wakes up and either tells the police it was you, or he comes after you hisself, then what?! I'm yo' man and you not lettin' me protect you. I *can't* protect you if you keep doin' this stupid shit. I want that muthafucka dead too but you can't be so reckless. You can't go around beatin' on people then just sit back and wait for the shit to hit the fan." He was makin' perfect sense, but then, he normally did. I finally felt nervous. What if he died? Did I really wanna become a murderer? Or did I just wanna beat some ass?

I broke down and told Isaiah everything. He had to take me out on the back porch so that Lil Rell wouldn't hear me, I was so upset. But Isaiah held me while I flipped out, letting me know I should've opened up and trusted him from the beginning. I couldn't help but think that, had I chosen him instead of Derrick to begin with, then I wouldn't be in the situation I was in. But he reminded me that Derrick was who he was. If he hadn't gotten me one way, he would've just gone to plan B. That's what scared the shit outta me. He knew I wasn't dead. And I knew he had a plan B, C, and probably D.

11

It had been two weeks since the detectives had paid me a visit, and the silence was killing me. I figured they would've called if Derrick had died and they would've come back and arrested me if he had run his mouth. I assumed the bastard was still kickin' and plottin' against me. Had I not been so preoccupied with my own thoughts, I wouldn't have answered my phone when it rang. I never answer calls I don't know. But I was off my game.

"Hello?"

"You have a collect call from... This Tasha! JaLea pick up!" she blurted out in the couple of seconds she had. I rolled my eyes, irritated as hell, and hung up. She must've lost her damn mind. Why in the world would she think I wanted to hear from her? She shoulda known I was lyin' when I offered to put money on her books for givin' up Derrick's name, if that's what she was calling for. Oh well, her fault. And how the hell did she get my damn number!?

Lil Rell ran up to me singing the ABC's and I couldn't help but sing with him. When I heard the front door opening, I knew it was Isaiah, so I twirled around so he could start singing with us. The look on his face was crazy though. He looked like he was about to throw up.

"Hi, Mr. Zay!" Lil Rell yelled.

"Hey, Rell." His response was so dry it pissed me off. I told Lil Rell to go to his room and watched as Isaiah hung his jacket up. He walked over to me and gave me a skeet, dry lip kiss on the cheek, and went and plopped down on the couch. I followed him.

"Wassup wit'chu?" I asked him. He clasped his fingers together and exhaled.

"Erica called my mama. She's in labor." I sucked my teeth and played with my nails a lil' bit, tryin' to figure out what the hell he was tellin' me for.

"Sooo..." He was taking too long to respond.

"Nobody is there wit' her-"

"*And*?!" I was tryin' not to get too pissed off. Lately, my anger had become its own person. He looked away from me and I got up to stand in his line of sight. "Did you lie to me?!" I yelled with my hands on my hips.

"What'chu mean, did I lie to you?"

"Is it really your baby?"

"Hell naw that ain't my baby!"

"Hell naw," Lil Rell mocked. I shot him an ugly stare, making him scurry back to his room, and I started to whisper.

"So why do you and yo' mama care if Erica is in labor?" I couldn't, for the life of me, understand why we were havin' this conversation.

"I don't care about Erica in the way you're thinking."

"Oh, really? So how do you care about her then?"

"We were together for a minute, and that was mainly because I couldn't be wit' you-"

"Don't blame me for you fuckin' Erica!" I turned away and he jumped up to grab my arms, and bent down in my face.

"I need you to listen to me and understand me, ok." He waited for me to nod. "Me and Erica were cool, but she was just a way to try and get over you and it didn't work. I thought she was gonna have my baby, but she lied to me. That pushed her further away from me. And you were hurt..." His voice trailed off a little. "I love you, JaLea. Erica was just a fling, but it's still fucked up that she don't have nobody. That don't mean I want her. It don't mean I wanna be her baby daddy, it just means I'm not an asshole." I looked down at the floor. He got on my damn nerves.

"Well it's apparent that since you brought it up that you wanna go, so go." He dropped his hands from my shoulders.

"Did you not hear anything I just said."

"Oh I heard you perfectly fine." I folded my arms. He could tell me all he wanted that Erica didn't mean anything to him, but it was obvious that she felt differently. He huffed and kissed me on my cheek, then he was gone. I was past heated. I shoulda told his friendly ass to stay home. But I was being stupid, and stubborn, and told him to go ahead, and now I needed a way to get rid of my anger. Almost as if by instinct, I picked up the phone and called Kim.

"Hello?" She sounded all chipper and shit. I planned on shuttin' that down real quick.

"Hey, *Kim*!" I said wit' an attitude.

"JaLea, what's wrong?" she asked, sounding a lil' irritated.

"What do you think is wrong? Erica calls and you send Isaiah runnin' to her?"

"I'm not sure what you're implying-"

"Oh you know exactly what I'm implying. You're tryin' to break me and Isaiah up!"

"Why would I-"

"I'm not stupid. I know you don't want us together."

"JaLea, I love you like a daughter."

"So I'm good enough to be your *daughter*, just not by bein' with your *son*."

"You're being paranoid-"

"Paranoid!? Oh please, Kim! Admit you think I'm damaged goods. You don't think I'm good enough for him!"

"I worry about you, sweetie." She was talkin' so calmly it was pissin' me off more. "I care about your well-being. Initially, I was a little bothered by you and Isaiah having a relationship because I looked at you as my *child*. But I always felt there was more between the two of you. I know my son cares for you very much, and he's a strong enough man to see you through the things you're going through. You know and I know that I'd never try and come between that. Maybe you're the one who doesn't think you're good enough for him." I hung up on her. She flipped the script on me and got on my damn nerves. I couldn't stand to be read like that! I couldn't help but wonder though, if she was right.

12

I paced the floor like a mad woman. In all my stubbornness, I couldn't bring myself to call Isaiah, even though I wanted to blow his phone up. Erica could be in labor for an hour or even until the next day. How dare he leave! How dare he wanna be with her while she was having her baby! I thought about what he had said, that he wasn't an asshole. Then I thought about what his mama said, that maybe I was the one who thought Isaiah was too good for me. I was completely torn. Should I have been proud of him for being the bigger person and not leaving Erica by herself? Hell, I should've gone with him, just to be petty. *No!* That was my problem, I was too damn spiteful. Erica hadn't done anything to me, up until she charged me at my party. But that was because she thought I was the one being shady. She didn't have a clue that the only reason I wasn't with Isaiah was because I could never have left Terrell for him. She had never known about my feelings.

My mind was clicking overtime. I had never been this jealous of Erica before. Yea, I was hurt when I thought they were messin' around a few years back, but this baby had me way too far in my feelings. The damn thing wasn't even mine, or Isaiah's, so he claimed. The thought of him being with her at a time like this was killing me. Child birth was an intimate, bonding experience, the most memorable in most women's lives. I thought about Terrell squeezing my hand, wiping my sweat, rubbing my head, coaching me through the pain, whispering how he loved me. He made me feel like the strongest woman in the world, and the inkling that Isaiah was being anywhere near sweet to Erica had all types of anxiety building up in my chest. It felt like I had acid reflux, I was so disturbed. I went in to lay with Lil Rell, hoping it would make me feel better. I played in his hair while he was asleep, and kept looking at my phone waiting for a call, a text, a poke on Facebook, *anything*. I ended up calling Mesha.

"Tell me I'm being ignorant or selfish." I waited after I told her what was going on.

"Now you know you called the *wrong* one! Hell naw you ain't bein' ignorant or selfish! If anything, you retarded as hell for lettin' his ass go. I woulda been like 'um, no sir, you gon' sit right here and look at me while I look at this t.v.'. That woulda been the end of it. Don't neither one of y'all owe her a damn thing."

"That's what I wanted to tell him, but then he started on this oh I don't wanna be an asshole and blah, blah, blah-"

"Be an asshole why? Because they were havin' sex and now she's about to have a baby that ain't even his? Who's is it anyway?"

"I don't know and I don't care."

"Mmhmm you need to be caring before she turn around and change her mind again. And she just the type of chick to do some lowdown crap like that." I rolled my eyes.

"Ain't no way she can pull that off. If it was his she woulda been due in the middle of June, not the beginning of May."

"I guess-" my line clicking cut Mesha off. My heart flipped at seeing Isaiah's face.

"Finally, I'mma call you back, this is him."

"Ok, and find out who the daddy is because inquiring minds wanna know!"

"Girl bye," I laughed and clicked over. "Well, hello," I answered with an attitude.

"Please don't be mad at me, Lea. One of her cousins is here so I'm on my way home." The way he said *home* did something to me. Yea, he had a key, but he also still had his own place. We hadn't discussed moving in with one another, but I knew it was sure to come up sometime soon.

I was so anxious when I heard his car pull up that I stood right by the door and scared him when he opened it. I apologized quickly and tapped my foot as he took his wallet and keys and sat them on the counter. It was like he was stalling. It wasn't dark at all yet, but he knew he had been gone a good five hours, so that mouth should've started running as soon as he walked through the door.

"Oh my God you gon' make me yank it outta you?" He exhaled and turned to face me.

"You were right, it was a bad idea," he said. I fought the urge to smile, but it didn't work. I tried to twist my mouth so he wouldn't notice, but he shook his head at me anyway. "As soon as I got there, she wanted a hug. I gave her one, but she wanted attention and affection and all I wanted to do was be there for moral support, since she didn't have anybody else. But she started talkin' shit-"

"Talkin' shit like *what*?"

"Like can I forgive her for lyin', can we try again, just give her another chance." I had wanted to call him out on giving her a hug, but I decided to let him finish until he said that.

"Oh, that bitch lost her mind. She knew what the hell she was doing when she called Kim wit' her trifling, sneaky ass. She knew y'all would feel sorry for her and you would more than likely come runnin'-"

"JaLea-"

"JaLea nothin'. I already didn't like her ass, but then she tries to go behind my back and do this shit. She beggin' to get her ass kicked!"

"Just know I put her in her place ok, baby. I made her call somebody to come and be with her because she hadn't. She didn't have the baby yet, I left as soon as her cousin got there." I only half heard what he said. My palms were tingling, wanting a piece of Erica. I pasted a smile on my face and looked at him.

"All that matters is that you came back *here*. You are too sweet for your own good." I hugged him, sinking into his chest. He just didn't know, his honesty had me seeing red. I'd give Erica a little while to recover, then I was on her ass.

13

I wheeled G-mama out into the yard so we wouldn't be cooped up inside. Her hair had gotten so long it was hanging well past her shoulders. I was so ashamed that it had been so long since I had been to visit her. I was much too preoccupied with my own feelings of revenge and hate. I looked around the yard and gave Terrell a silent thank you. Had it not been for him, there was no telling where my G-mama would be. I knew we wouldn't have gotten a dime if it had been left to Mr. Charles.

"It's good to see you looking so healthy G-mama," I started. She stared out, looking through flowers. Even though I figured she didn't understand a word I was saying, I still felt like crap for bullshittin' her. I broke down and told her everything. I apologized for being in bed with the enemy, even letting him into my life. It didn't matter that I didn't know who he was at the time, the only thing that stuck in my mind was the fact that I had *done* it. I told her everything I did, beating up Theresa and Derrick, lying to everybody, letting hate consume me. I told her how crazy I felt, not to say anything bad about her. Lord knows I wouldn't know how to act if somebody took Lil Rell from me the way they took my mama from G-mama. I had just been so damn upset! I was stuttering and in tears by the time I finished and had to get some tissue from my purse to wipe my nose.

"Stop." I almost broke my neck looking at G-mama. I thought I was trippin' at first because I was blowing my nose. But I wasn't trippin'. She had said stop, clear as day. I looked around trying to see If anybody had moved within earshot. Of course, there was nobody else close enough.

"G-mama?" I smiled in her face, though she didn't smile back. "Stop what? Being mad, trying to get revenge, taking my anger out on people?" I searched her eyes frantically. "Can you say something else?" I wrapped my arms around hers and rested my head on her shoulder. I begged for almost another hour. The nurses had to make me let her go eat. I didn't appreciate the looks they gave me when I told them she had spoken. They couldn't even tell me definitively what was wrong with her, so how could they know for a fact that she would never speak again? I had always had faith that one day I'd hear her voice again. Since I had, I was so hesitant to leave her. The only thing that caused me to turn away was my phone vibrating in my purse.

"Isaiah! Guess what!" I couldn't contain myself.

"Wassup, babe." He was dry as hell, but nothing could get me down.

"My G-mama talked!"

"She did?!" He perked up. "What did she say?"

"She said 'stop'."

"Stop?" he asked, sounding confused.

"I was telling her about everything that went on, everything I did, and she just said 'stop'. The nurses think I'm crazy but I *heard* her!"

"I believe you, baby." His tone was weird.

"What's wrong, Isaiah?"

"Nothin', I'll talk to you when you get home. Spend time with your grandma."

"They took her to eat. What's goin' on?" He was quiet on the other end, making me nervous.

"Somebody broke in again."

~~~

I zoomed through the streets, praying I wouldn't get a ticket. I couldn't believe it. My head was pounding thinking about somebody in my house again! Of course, my first thought was Derrick. The police hadn't said two words to me since they left my house questioning me about putting him in the hospital. I call, then have to leave messages which nobody returns. It was bullshit. I had no idea whether Derrick was dead or alive, in custody or free to roam around breaking in people's houses. I tried to stay calm, since my G-mama had told me to stop, whatever that meant. My own interpretation was to stop trippin' off of revenge. But damn, what was I supposed to do, just let people run all over me?

The police beat me home. A sick wave of déjà vu hit me as I walked into my ransacked apartment. Isaiah was standing in the middle of the room talking to two officers and there was shit everywhere. There was only one thing of value that I still had in my apartment since the first break in. I ran to Lil Rell's room where I had moved the picture of me, him, and his daddy. His bed was on its side, all his lil' pictures had been yanked off the walls, his lamp was knocked over, dresser drawers were pulled out and clothes were everywhere. I searched for a good two minutes until I found the picture, not even realizing that Isaiah and the police were staring at me. I glared at the officers and sat the picture in a drawer before I returned to the living room.

Of course, they had the same questions as everybody else. *Do you have any idea who would do this? Was anything of value taken? Does anyone else have a key?*

"Damn, do the police not talk to each other at all? Y'all don't know y'all have been here before, numerous times? It's the same people. Is Derrick Meyer out of the hospital?" The officers looked at me like I was crazy. "Is *Anthony Merritt* out of the hospital?" This time, they looked at each other. "You know what," I walked towards the front door. "Get out."

"Excuse me ma'am?" one of the officers asked.

"You heard me. Y'all are just here for fun because it's obvious you aren't doing anything productive. I know who did it, you know who did it, but y'all still here asking questions." They scooted uneasily out the door and I slammed it behind them. I fished Detective Dixon's card out of my purse and, of course, had to leave a message. "I was assaulted by Anthony Merritt and in a coma for over a month. Y'all had him and apparently didn't do anything wit' him because guess what, he's fuckin' wit' me again. Or he got his people fuckin' wit' me. Either way, if anything happens to me or anybody I care about because y'all didn't do y'all job, I'mma make sure the badges get sued off you bastards!" I hung up, only half satisfied, and plopped down on the couch with my leg shaking uncontrollably. Isaiah sat beside me and put his hand on my knee and I immediately started feeling bad. He knew I had demons, but I'm sure he wasn't happy about having to deal with them all. I was tempted to tell him that he could leave if it was too much, when he put his arm around my shoulder.

"You were right before. I see now we just gon' have to take care of these muthafuckas ourselves."

14

"**Y**'all asses gon' have to move!" Mesha was loud, as always. I almost spilled my Kool-Aid all over her couch when she yelled in my ear. "I used to talk to this real estate agent-"

"And let them run me outta my house? I don't think so!"

"Stop tryin' to be hard! Whoever Derrick got runnin' up in yo' house knows exactly where you are. You don't know who it is or where they are, but they know exactly where to find you. It ain't like you broke and can't move."

"*And*! Me and Isaiah gon' take care of things."

"Oh really? And who are y'all? Black Bonnie and Clyde? *Take care of things*... what does that even *mean*?"

"Exactly what it sounds like!"

"Boo you know I'mma ride wit'chu through whatever. I'm all for beatin' some ass, but I ain't killin' nobody. I already told you that. The most I'll do is drive yo' ass home and act like I ain't see shit. But is that what you really want? Because that's what it seems like it's gon' have to come down to if y'all keep it up. You and Derrick just gon' keep fuckin' wit' each other 'til somebody give up? Who you think gon' surrender first?"

"He killed Terrell, Mesha-"

"And I understand that. What I'm askin' you is do *you* wanna be a killer, too?" I stared at her, unsure of the answer. Yes, beating Theresa and Derrick's ass had felt so good, but how would I have felt if one of them had died? Could I really kill Derrick? Could I kill my son's grandmama?! I thought about the way I felt when I was swinging that bat, and my decision was made.

"When it comes to Derrick, I'm a different person. There is nobody in this world, outside of his brother, that can make me feel the kind of hate I feel. Every time I think about him, my chest starts hurting." I rubbed my scar through my shirt. "Can you imagine how often that is?" Mesha's eyes softened.

"I just don't want you to do something you'll regret. You or Isaiah."

"Believe me sis, when it happens, regret is the last thing I'mma feel."

~~~

"Good morning, JaLea!" The secretary at G-mama's facility seemed extra chipper. I figured she must've got some the night before or something, until she came from behind the counter and put her arm around me. "I hear your granny has been asking for you this morning." I looked at her in disbelief and she had the biggest grin on her face.

"Asking for me? Like-"

"Saying your *name*." My eyes welled up with tears and I almost broke down in the middle of the lobby. In the past few days, she seemed to be more alert and watching me when I talked to her, but I wasn't ready for that. I couldn't get to her fast enough. She was in the common area since they had just finished breakfast. She was at a window, facing out into the garden. My heart started racing. It had been two weeks since she had spoken the first time. I knew at first the staff had thought I was crazy. I had almost begun to think it was a fluke. I stooped between her and the window and she looked directly at me and said my name like she had been saying it for all these years.

"Hi G-mama." I smiled and she smiled back at me! I couldn't do anything but lay my head in her lap and cry. I cried for the nearly eight years that were stolen from her. I cried for the daughter she lost, the mother I lost, and I cried for the time she missed with Lil Rell. I cried for the hell I went through with Tasha because my G-mama wasn't able to be there for me. I started to feel the hate boil in my stomach. It was like acid eating away at me. I looked up and G-mama was still focused on me. She looked so content and at peace. I had to get up and stand behind her to try and regain some control.

"JaLea! How are you?" I spun around, startled. G-mama's head nurse was grinning at me. "It's good to see you."

"It's good to see you too, Nurse Pollar," I beamed. I kissed G-mama on the forehead and followed the nurse into a conference room where she told me what I had been waiting years to hear.

"Well, she's finally coming around." I exhaled and closed my eyes. "I told you before that I've seen a number of cases where patients suffer from mental breaks brought on by severe depression, heartbreak and stress. Your grandmother experienced all of those things and went into a shell. Honestly, I was starting to fear that she'd never come out. She's been doing some moving, a little more each day. Any movement, especially after so long, is a jolt in the right direction, but she *fed* herself a little today. It wasn't for long, but it's still progress." I sat and listened to Nurse Pollar talk about my G-mama, feeling like she was talking about somebody else. Even though I had never lost hope, it was almost impossible to believe that she was coming back to me.

"When can I take her home?" I was ready for her to get out of that place. They had taken excellent care of her over the years, true enough, but I would feel much better having her with me.

"Well, we wouldn't want to move too fast," she laughed. "She is progressing at an alarming rate, almost teaching herself. We'd want to keep her monitored still, take her through some more physical therapy, make sure she stays on a progressive upward slope so we're confident that when she leaves we aren't letting her go prematurely." I nodded, excited about what I was hearing. The wheels in my head started turning, trying to figure out how I would take care of her once she was out.

I hugged the nurse and visited with my G-mama for a little while longer. It was so refreshing that when I talked to her, she actually paid attention and nodded. I couldn't wait to call Aaron and let him know. The facility made sure to let me know how great my dad had been while I was 'sick'.

"Hey, sweetie," he answered the phone laughing.

"What's going on?" I asked him.

"Nothin'." He kept giggling like a school girl.

"*You did it!*" I immediately recognized Kim's voice laughing in the background. I hadn't spoken to her since she lightweight went off on me about Isaiah.

"But y'all ain't together?" I asked Aaron with an attitude. I didn't *want* to care what the hell they were doing, I just hated being lied to. And I hated the fact that he was runnin' through my mama's old friends and they were just letting him do it, like she had never existed.

"We are just *friends*, JaLea-"

"Friends my ass," I yelled and hung up.

15

I drove to Kim's house, way too far in my feelings. I was determined to find out what was going on between her and Aaron. I had to laugh at myself a little bit. I had gotten a nasty attitude with her because of how I assumed she felt about me and Isaiah, yet here I was on my way to go off about her and my dad. I shrugged it off though. My reasons for being upset trumped hers any day. I pulled up and tried my best to knock without as much attitude as I felt.

"Hey, Jalea!" Kim was overly excited when she answered the door. I wanted to snap on her, but my heart wouldn't let me. It was *Kim*. I mumbled hello and stepped past her.

"Is my dad still here?" I asked.

"Hey, Jalea," Aaron came into the living room from the kitchen.

"So wassup?" I wanted to know.

"Can you sit down so we can talk for a minute?" Kim asked. I huffed and took a seat on the love seat. They sat across from me on the couch. "Jalea, I'm going to say this as plainly and calmly as I can. Your dad and I have been friends for a very long time. A lot has gone on recently that has made us closer friends, but we are not sleeping together. We're simply enjoying each other's company."

"And that ain't gon' lead to y'all sleeping together?" I asked.

"If it does?" Aaron cut in. Both Kim and I shot eyes at him. "Sweetie, Kim and I are both grown. We're havin' this conversation because you seem upset by the fact that we're spending time together. We're older-"

"You're forty!"

"And forty-year-olds need love too-" I held my hand up in his face, not wanting to hear it.

"Jalea, I think what your father is trying to say is that we have the right to spend time together and let it be our business. Whatever we do or don't do is our business. We're having this conversation with you to try and ease some of your fears-"

"Ease some of my fears? I'm not scared, I'm pissed off! You can't fuck nobody but my mama friends?"

"You need to watch your mouth, JaLea Washington-"

"For who? You?"

"Yes!" Aaron yelled. "For me *and* for her!"

"Whatever-"

"She was there for you when your mother and I couldn't be." I slung my purse back over my shoulder and was headed for the door, but Aaron grabbed me. "Look, I know I haven't been the best father-"

"You got that right," I sneered at him.

"Jalea you are the reason I cleaned myself up. You don't understand what it's like to be so depressed that you feel you have nowhere to turn but drugs."

"Oh my God, I learned about sayin' no to drugs in elementary school. I certainly don't need a pep talk from you."

"This isn't a pep talk. This is a long overdue conversation. A long overdue apology." I resisted the urge to look up at him. Stubbornness at its finest. "Jalea, I am sorry for the childhood that you didn't have. I should've been the one to help you pick up the pieces all those years ago, and I wasn't. I couldn't realize how much you were hurting because I was too selfish and focusing on numbing my own pain." I looked up at him, and saw the hurt and regret in his eyes. "Since you lost Terrell, I vowed that I wouldn't be another person you lost. As much as you hate me, I'd like to think that deep down you really do love me.

"I don't hate you," I told him. That made him smile.

"I know you have a lot of pinned up anger and aggression. Please don't take it out on Kim. She's pitched in as much as anybody, if not more to help with Lil Rell when you were away. She helped me keep my head on straight when I wanted to start numbing the pain again. It was so hard seeing my baby like that. Kim was comforting, and caring, and understanding because she loves you too. Nobody is tryin' to hide anything from you. Nobody is tryin' to be sneaky and go behind your back. Nobody is tryin' to get together to keep you from Isaiah-"

"Wait, what?!" I yelled. Kim laughed and punched Aaron in the arm.

"Oh don't act like you weren't thinking it," she replied. I gave her the side eye.

"You don't know me!"

"But we do though," Aaron laughed. I wanted to be cool and not still have an attitude, but in the back of my mind, it was still messed up. They'd end up fuckin'. I was sure of it. And it irritated the hell outta me for so many reasons. The sound of the doorbell snapped me out of my trance. Kim excused herself and went to answer and as soon as she looked through the blinds, I cocked my head. Her body language was setting off all types of alarms. She stiffened, dropped her hands to her sides, and looked at the floor.

"What is it, Kim?" Aaron asked. She looked at me and bit her bottom lip, seeming nervous.

"Jalea, I want you to stay calm, ok." My heart started beating fast and the doorbell rang again. I knew exactly who it was, so I took my purse off and settled on the love seat, making sure I looked comfortable as hell, before Kim opened the door.

"Hi, Erica! I forgot you were stopping by today!" She sounded genuinely happy to see her, which pissed me off. I had to fight myself not to laugh at Aaron who had scooted to the corner with his eyes wide, like he was about to watch a huge fight. Since Isaiah had convinced me it wasn't his baby, I had put that trick on the back burner. I had bigger fish to fry.

"Hi, Kim!" She came in with a pumpkin seat and baby bag and leaned into Kim for a hug. The look on her face when saw me was priceless. I should've had my damn phone out to catch the expression. She was scared, nervous, and confused all at the same time. I waved at her, just to be petty. She had tried me on my birthday with that lucky ass sucker punch. She had tried me while Isaiah was at the hospital with her, taking his kindness for weakness and acting like she didn't give a damn he was with me. I had half a mind to be real disrespectful and drag her ass all through Kim's house, but I wouldn't do it. Not right then, anyway. But I couldn't ignore my itchy palms for long. "I can come back later-"

"Oh no, you can stay," I grinned at her. "I was just about to leave." I knew it burned her up that it seemed like I was calling the shots. I made it my business to look over in the pumpkin seat just to make myself feel better. If I saw a yellow baby with green eyes, I was gonna scream. She was a lil' chocolate girl, though. "Cute," I commented. "You leavin' wit' me?" I asked Aaron. He nodded, eager to get away from the drama. I winked at Erica on my way out, feeding the fire a little. I heard Aaron stifle a laugh behind me and Kim swatted him on his shoulder. I waited until we got in the car and started bugging up.

We actually had a decent ride to his house. I hadn't expected the visit to Kim's to go the way it had, and talking to him kept my mind off why the hell Erica would be paying her a visit anyway. I had a checklist of things to do after my visit with my G-mama that day and wanted to get going. Call it woman's intuition, but something told me to stop by my house first. My heart was beating fast, thinking about Derrick jumping out from behind the door and grabbing me soon as I walked in. It was a shame I was scared to walk through my own front door, but I switched the light on as quick as I could, and found Theresa sprawled out on my living room floor.

16

I blinked more than a few times. I had to be trippin'. I couldn't be seeing what I thought I was seeing. Theresa was stretched out in my floor halfway under the coffee table, in just a bra and capri pants. I slammed the front door thinking it would scare her, but she didn't budge.

"Theresa!" I bent over her and yelled her name but she still didn't move a muscle. I nudged her with my foot until I finally got a Nike up under her side and turned her over onto her back. It barely felt like she weighed eighty pounds. She still didn't wake up. "Shit!" I panicked. My mind was racing. What the hell was she doing in my house?! How did she get in?! What in God's name happened that she ended up under my coffee table half naked?! I pulled out my phone and called the police. I had the perfect opportunity to stick it to her ass, but I wasn't about to beat on an unconscious woman, especially not in my own house. Once I got off with them, I called Isaiah.

"Where are you?" I asked in a slight panic.

"I'm around the corner. What's wrong?"

"Theresa is laid out in the middle of the living room floor!" I answered him.

"What?!" he yelled.

"Yea you heard me. I came home and this hoe is passed out in the floor in her damn bra!"

"What the fuck?"

"I don't know what the hell is goin' on, but I called the police already. They should be able to get here wit' they eyes closed by now," I joked. Less than five minutes later, Isaiah was pulling up with the police, an ambulance, and a fire truck on his tail. I hated the neighbors standing around like it was a damn movie. I know they were probably thinkin' 'what happened this time?' I was tired of having the police at my house.

"She's right through the door?" an EMT worker asked walking up on the porch. I nodded at him and grabbed Isaiah's hand as soon as I could to pull him inside. His eyes bugged out of his head when he saw her. Another paramedic rushed in past us and they started working on her, pumping her chest and everything. I couldn't believe my eyes. I felt shady as hell for thinkin' the bitch better not had overdosed on my floor. They needed to get her out of there with a quickness!

"And we meet again?" I spun around, immediately recognizing one of the officers that had come to the first couple of break-ins.

"Officer Bass!" It was nice to see a familiar face. I was so tired of telling and retelling the same damn story, I didn't know what to do.

"So, we didn't get a chance to find Theresa before she found you, huh?" she asked. Isaiah threw his arm on my shoulder for support.

"I really don't know what's goin' on at this point," I told her. "I came home and found my mother-in-" The words stopped short in my throat and Isaiah's hand tightened a little on my shoulder. "I found my son's grandmother layin' on the floor. She doesn't have a key so I don't know how she got in. You know I always assumed she played a part in the break-ins but this..." I swung my arm towards where the paramedics were trying to revive Theresa. "This I can't believe." As soon I finished speaking, she was coughing and spitting and trying to scoot away from everyone. I let out a sigh of relief as we watched as the paramedics try to calm her confused ass down.

"Leave me alone!" was all she kept screaming as they fought to get her on the stretcher and strap her down. I had so many questions for her, but the officers had questions for me.

"They have to take her to the hospital to monitor her, see what the problem is-"

"Oh, I know exactly what the problem is. She overdosed on my floor." Officer Bass acted like I hadn't said anything and kept going.

"My partner and I are gonna tail them to the E.R. so we can question her when she's able. You're welcome to follow."

"We'll be there." Isaiah answered for me and I thanked her as she left. "I don't wanna be here," I told Isaiah once everybody had pulled off. "I don't wanna sleep in this apartment another night."

"You know my door is always open." Isaiah hugged me. Although we spent plenty of nights together, we each still had our own space. We had never really talked about moving in together and I appreciated the gesture, but I was in a different mind frame. Lil Rell was getting bigger, I wanted him to have his own backyard, my G-mama was almost ready to come home and she needed space too. "So," he started. I pulled back and looked up at him.

"Wassup?" I asked.

"Mother-in-law?" I closed my eyes. I figured that would come back to bite me in the ass, but I didn't think he'd bring it up so soon.

"It just slipped out." I understood where he was coming from, but it irritated me that he wanted to talk about my wording instead of a woman damn near dying on the floor. He nodded and grinned at me.

"I know it's not a good time." He laughed a little, making me think he was nervous. I'd hate for him to think he had to compete with Terrell, God rest his soul. I didn't wanna think about that though.

"Yea, we can talk about it later. Right now though, we need to get to the hospital."

I couldn't wait to hear what Theresa had to say. Her crackhead ass had better been talkin' too. I needed answers, and I needed them now. The E.R. acted like she was royalty or some shit since she came in with police, tryin' to be all secretive about her room. Luckily Officer Bass was walking past and took us to the back. Standing outside Theresa's room, looking in on her, she seemed so much smaller, if that was even possible.

"She couldn't wait to talk and put the blame on someone else." Officer Bass snapped me out of my trance. "Do you know an Erica Sanders?"

17

"**H**ell yea, I know Erica!" Isaiah grabbed my arm to shut me up, but I couldn't keep my composure. "She had something to do with the break-ins at my house?"
"Calm down, JaLea-"
"Calm down!?" I yelled at him. "Calm down for what? I am tired of these people fuckin' wit' me, ok!"
"I know, baby, but let's just hear what Officer Bass has to say and see where we go from there." I had to take a few deep breaths before I calmed down. I crossed my arms, ready to hear what the story was.
"Ok?" Officer Bass asked and I nodded my head. "It's one hell of a story she's telling. She claims an old friend of hers, Tasha, introduced her to a young man who wanted to punish you for his brother being locked up. Says he had her start off doing little things, then started paying her and getting drugs for her to do more. She

showed him where you stay and whenever he felt like it, he'd pick the lock and send her and her friends in to ransack your place a little. She thought it was fun and admitted she doesnt like you." If I hadn't been so pissed off, I would've laughed. "She thinks you had something to do with her son being murdered." I rolled my eyes.

"She's crazy as hell," I complained. "Derrick, who she let talk her into doin' all this crap, is the one who killed her son. And I know exactly where to find Erica's ass. Them Sanders can kiss my ass!" Officer Bass's eyes got big and she started jotting something down in her notebook.

"You say this Derrick killed your ex fiance'? How do you know this?" I paused and Isaiah rubbed my neck.

"Might as well tell her everything, babe." The three of us sat down and I filled her in on everything that had happened. By the time I finished, it seemed like she had gone through every sheet in her notebook.

"I am so sorry about everything you've been through." She seemed genuinely apologetic. "I know all of these officers and detectives that have been handling things for you-"

"Supposed to be handling things for me," I cut in.

"You said it. I didn't," she laughed. "In my defense, it's extremely hard to find people like Theresa. The streets rarely talk. And I've been looking for a *Derrick Meyers* for months. Nobody informed of this new information." I shook my head.

"I know, all this sounds crazy, but what's gonna happen now? And what did she say about Erica?"

"Well as soon as they release Theresa, she's gonna be escorted to the station for breaking and entering and property damage, and we're looking to question Erica to see what she has to say. Apparently, this last time, Erica gave her a key to go in and take some things, but, as you can see, Theresa just wasn't up to it."

"How did she even get a key?!" I yelled. Isaiah rubbed my arm.

"That's what we need to find out." I didn't hesitate to give Officer Bass the address of the Sanders' house, and Kim's address, just in case she was still there. I thought she looked shook when she saw me because she knew I wanted to beat her ass about my man, but it could've easily been because she knew what the hell she had done.

Isaiah and I were headed to his car when my phone rang. "It's yo' mama," I told him. "I didn't even get to tell you about what happened at her house." I didn't give him a chance to respond before I answered. "Hey Kim."

"JaLea are you busy? I need to talk to you."

"Oh Lord, last time you needed to talk to me, you dropped the bomb about Tasha. Wassup?"

"It's about what Erica came over to talk to me about."

"Oh, that she gave her auntie a key to my place to steal from me? I found Theresa passed out on my living room floor."

"Oh, Jesus..."

"Yea, oh Jesus is right. So she came to you to confess?"

"She wanted me to talk to you and tell you what was going on. She knows, given your strained relationship with her-"

"Strained? Hmph, I wonder why?"

"JaLea!" she yelled at me.

"Ok!" I yelled back. Isaiah stared at me, refusing to start the car until he knew what was going on.

"She's being threatened-"

"Oh, this sounds vaguely familiar." Kim huffed on the other end. "I'm sorry, go ahead."

"Her child's father is threatening to take her daughter."

"What does her baby daddy drama have to do with me though?"

"Her child's father is Derrick."

18

"What?!" I yelled into the receiver. I didn't know whether to curse because the heffa went behind my back, laugh because she messed around and got pregnant by the nutcase, or be scared because he had yet another person to use to get to me.

"What?" Isaiah asked.

"Derrick is Erica's baby daddy!" I told him. He squinted his eyes and shook his head at me. I nodded back at him and put Kim on speaker. "How did that even happen?" I asked.

"She met him a while ago and they were kind of on again, off again. She had no idea the two of you knew each other until you all were at Isaiah's party."

"I guess that didn't stop her, huh?" I joked.

"I understand your frustration, JaLea-"

"Oh, I'm not frustrated. I was frustrated about Isaiah. Pissed the hell off to be exact, but Derrick? I'm not frustrated at all. It's funny. I don't know what she thought she was doin', but I see she got much more than what she bargained for."

"After details started coming out about what happened to you, she felt horrible."

"Did she feel stupid too?" I asked.

"She's paying an ultimate price for what she did JaLea, isn't that enough?!" I couldn't believe she yelled at me like that. I looked over at Isaiah who was focused on the road, like he hadn't heard anything.

"You always wanna save somebody, don't you? Anybody who's in need, no matter if they set somebody up to be killed, they're a recovering crack head, or they got pregnant by a deranged psychopath, you're gonna bend over backwards to treat 'em with kid gloves." I didn't even look in Isaiah's direction. I knew he was shooting daggers at me with those eyes.

"What's wrong with showing a little sympathy, Jalea? Maybe you need to learn that the world isn't black and white. I'm sure you've done things that you aren't proud of. And I'm sure you wouldn't want the people who you care about to shut you out or treat you like a leper because you messed up." I wanted to go clean off, but I knew she was right. No matter how mad at her I was for listening to Erica's problems, if she ever found out that Derrick killed Terrell, I'd still want her to look at me the same as she always did. That was the main reason it was so hard to tell anybody but the police at first. Erica had admitted her faults when I couldn't.

"Nothing is wrong with it, Kim. I'm just in a different head space when it comes to her and Derrick and Theresa and everybody who messed me over."

"I need you to listen to me because Erica is scared."

"Why didn't she go to the police?" I interrupted.

"Not too long after she got home with the baby, he popped up at the Sanders house. She doesn't know how he got in. All of a sudden, he was just there. He said he didn't care about the baby, but he'd take her if she didn't help him. She didn't ask any questions, she just did as she was told." I rolled my eyes.

"I'm sorry he's bein' like that, but she had time to go to the police and she didn't. She waited until Theresa came over and did exactly what he asked her to do so she's still on my shit list."

"Be that as it may, but that boy has a key to your apartment. He gave Erica one and no telling how many more copies he has." I closed my eyes trying to concentrate. Why the hell wasn't Derrick locked up? Why didn't the police let me know that the man I accused of attempted murder was free to roam St. Louis? How the hell did he get a copy of my house key?

"Ma," Isaiah cut in. "Did she say he had anything else up his sleeve?" Kim was quiet for a minute.

"Hello, Isaiah," she said, clearly irritated that she was on speakerphone.

"Hey, did she say anything about him having anything else planned?"

"No, she just wanted to protect her baby and was too scared to ask any questions. She assumed he just didn't like Jalea and was willing to do whatever to get to her." I laughed to myself wondering how everybody who didn't like me seemed to have formed their own lil' gang and just started wreckin' my life.

"Well the police might be stoppin' by your house lookin' for her. Theresa snitched on her, and I told the police that the last time I saw her, she was there.

"She's not here anymore, but fair enough," Kim responded. "Please protect yourselves and Lil Rell," she added. "That was my point of calling. I needed to let you know what was going on. Do you know what he has against you? What is his angle?" I huffed, ready to spill my guts, but I couldn't. Not over the phone at least. She needed to hear it in person, and before anybody else could tell her.

"You busy?" I asked, laughing. "I need one of those therapy sessions you been handing out." Isaiah slapped my arm, but turned in the direction of his mom's house.

~~~

Kim about passed out when I told her everything. Her mouth was hanging open through half of my story, but I knew if I didn't keep talking that I wouldn't make it through it.

"Let me get this straight," she responded once I finished. "Chris's brother has been stalking you for years waiting for the opportunity to get back at you for your mom, God rest her soul, protecting herself." I nodded. "He popped up at random places, started messing with your house and your cars and... Lord... killed Terrell once y'all got engaged, eased in where he made an opening, got Erica pregnant at some point during all of this, conned you out of ten thousand dollars, and when you found out what he was up to, he tried to kill you?"

"That about sums it up," Isaiah answered her. She nodded, keeping her eyes trained on the floor. We watched, almost scared to speak, as she wrung her hands together for a few seconds. She lifted her head and looked at us with pure hatred in her eyes that I had never seen from her before.

"So, what are we gonna do about it?"

19

"**D**id you see her face?!" I laughed as Isaiah and I drove away from Kim's house. "She was serious as hell! I can't imagine Kim throwin' 'em." I was buggin' up, but Isaiah was straight faced. "What's wrong?"
"What do you mean, what's wrong?!" he yelled. "Everything is wrong! And now my mama wants in on this bullshit too!"
"Excuse me if my life is bullshit-"
"No, JaLea, you will *not* pull that on me. Don't try and turn my words around when you know what I mean!" I crossed my arms and looked out the window. "The situation wit' that nigga Derrick is some bullshit. The fact that he ain't locked up is some bullshit. The fact that he's using Erica to get to you is some bullshit. And the fact that now my mama wanna try and do something since the police are draggin' their feet is some *bullshit*. If anything happens to my mama-"

"What makes you think something will happen to her?"

"What don't you get, JaLea? His ass is movin' through shadows. He always seems to be one step ahead of us-"

"Except for when I caught him outside his apartment." Isaiah threw me an evil glare and I shut up.

"As long as he's breathin', none of us are safe." I thought about what he said as we rode in silence. The thoughts that would run through your mind when your life is in danger. I was already feeling it, had been for a while. Isaiah saying that none of us were safe had really struck a chord in me. He was right. Derrick had proven that he would go above and beyond to get back at me for his brother being locked up, that included taking away people that I loved.

~~~

"Girl shut the fuck up!" Mesha jumped up and screamed. I slapped my hands over my ears.

"I need to wear ear plugs whenever I tell you some news." I rolled my eyes at her as Lil Rell ran around her living room.

"JaLea!" She leaned in front of me blocking the game I was playing on my phone and I pushed her away. "You can't drop bombs on me like that and expect me not to scream! Like what the fuck?! Wait. Let me process this shit."

"If my baby curse, I'mma slap you."

"Friend! This shit is gettin' crazier by the minute! You need to call Steve Harvey. He can have a whole show about yo' ass." I shook my head at her. "And what does holier than thou, miss goody-two-shoes Kim think she gon' do?"

"Girl, I don't know. And Isaiah is hot wit' me talkin' about how he don't want his mama anywhere near this mess."

"Do you blame him?!" Mesha asked. She had a point.

"Wouldn't it be a trip if one brother killed my mama and the other brother killed us?" Mesha looked at me with a blank face.

"Bitch, you need help," she commented as she slid on the floor to play with Lil Rell." Don't say no shit like that." I watched them, thinking about the missed time with my son. How could I not think negatively all the time? I was forced to look over my shoulder 24-7, paranoid all the time. I snatched my phone out of my purse. I might as well have had the SLPD on speed dial at that point. Officers and detectives were at my house more than anybody else, except maybe Theresa's dirty ass. No telling how many times she had been in there. I cringed at the thought. I didn't even wanna go back to pack things to take to Isaiah's place.

"What I need is closure. I need this to be over. If they all could just go away, then me, Lil Rell and Isaiah, and everybody else could live a normal life. Is that too much to ask for?" Before Mesha could answer, her phone rang. She glanced at it and rolled her eyes.

"Girl I do not do anonymous phone calls. They got me messed up!"

"Who man you messin' wit' now?" I joked, snatching the phone from her. She shook her head in protest as I answered. "Who is this?" I asked in my best side chick voice. There was a pause on the other end. "Hello?" I asked with an attitude.

"Wassup, lil' bitch?" Derrick's voice on the other end turned my blood ice cold.

"Why is this nigga callin' yo' phone?" I whispered to Mesha.

"What nigga?" Mesha snapped. I put the phone on speaker.

"Because I don't want you yet. I'mma pick off everybody one by one," he growled,

"Oh, hell no you won't!" Mesha yelled.

"Come outside and call my bluff." Mesha and I looked at each other, then at Lil Rell. Everything started moving in slow motion and the only thing I could hear was my own heart beating. I dropped the phone and grabbed Lil Rell. Mesha followed, pushing us towards the basement door. Every step I took vibrated through my entire body. As hard as I talked when it came to Derrick, I was scared shitless. Had he found out where Mesha stayed? Was he really outside? Was he really planning to try and eliminate everybody I loved? My fears became reality when gunshots rang out.

One... two... I counted the shots as Mesha screamed, slamming the basement door behind us.

"What the fuck?!" Three...four...five... Lil Rell started crying as we scrambled down the steps. Six... I tried to comfort him, but I could barely comfort myself. I tried bouncing him on my hip while Mesha paced in a corner cursing to herself and wringing her hands. "What are we gonna do? What the hell are we gonna do?" she asked. I shook my head at her. I had no clue. The shooting had stopped, for the moment, but I couldn't do anything but try to breath. My chest was heavy, my scar throbbed thinking about Derrick busting through the basement door and killing the three of us. He had the upper hand. I couldn't tell which direction the shooting had come from, I didn't know if he was still outside waiting. All I knew was that we were trapped in the basement with no phone. I had dropped Mesha's when we ran, and I left mine on the couch when I answered hers. We were sitting ducks!

"Mommy," Lil Rell whined. "Can we go home?"

"In a minute, baby," I whispered. That minute felt like hours. It turned out to only be about fifteen minutes until police were walking through the house calling out for whoever was there. I climbed the steps with Lil Rell and almost cried. I had never been happier to see the police in my life. Mesha came out behind me and I followed her to the living room where her front door was almost shot off the hinges. She covered her face, shaking her head, and I immediately saw red again. If we hadn't run to the basement, there was no telling if any of us would've been alive.

I reluctantly gave my statement. I got so tired of speaking his name. To the police, he was Anthony Merritt. To me, he was Derrick, a dead muthafucka if I ever got ahold of him. I knew exactly why he was free, my word against his, no evidence and that apartment probably wasn't even in either of the names he was using. His ass had spent years trying to get to me. He knew my every move, he knew everybody I knew, he knew every aspect of my life before he even decided to strike. He definitely had the upper hand. I wouldn't even bother the police anymore. I needed to suck it up, stop bein' a punk, and handle shit myself like I had planned when I was still in the hospital. No more beating around the bush.

20

"Why I gotta ask her?" Isaiah griped. The plan was to squeeze Erica for information on her baby daddy.

"Because she'll open up to you before she'll open up to me. I need to know how often he contacts her, what he's planning, who's all involved, and most importantly, where he's hiding." Isaiah huffed and crossed his arms. "You did see Mesha's door, didn't you? I was there with Lil Rell. The police coulda easily shown up to a homicide instead of an attempted one."

"Yea," he whispered. "I know."

"You were the one who said we won't be safe as long as he's breathing. He doesn't give a damn about repercussions. It was broad daylight, and I'm sure nobody saw a thing, as *usual*."

"I'll have her meet me at my mama house." I nodded and sucked my teeth. It was my idea, but I was still leery about them being together, even in Kim's presence. As much as I wanted to go with him, I had to trust my man. It was Erica who I didn't trust. I could see her balling her eyes out falling all in his lap wanting him to hold her and protect her and her baby. I wanted to punch something just thinkin' about it. I needed answers, though. I looked around at my room as I packed up, knowing I couldn't stay there anymore. It didn't even matter that it wasn't safe. Derrick had proven that he was one step ahead anyway. He more than likely knew where Isaiah stayed, but the visual of Theresa on my living room floor and the thought that she had been there before, probably numerous times... it made me sick to my stomach.

"I'll take Lil Rell to see G-mama and meet you back at your place. I don't expect you to be too long," I hinted with an attitude. He winked at me. I couldn't help but smile at him.

~~~

"She's improving steadily," the nurse whispered with a grin on her face. I stood in G-mama's doorway and watched her try to brush her hair. Her hand was a little shaky and the brush was barely doing anything, but she was trying. I smiled, thinking about the first time I tried to do my hair after I got out of the hospital. It was pretty much the same scene. Finally, she turned around and smiled at us.

"Ganny!" Lil Rell yelled. I let him run to her and crawl up in her lap.

"Rell," she said. My mouth dropped. She had always understood everything I said! I made sure Lil Rell knew exactly who she was even though there was a chance she'd never smile at him, hug him, or talk to him. The fact that she knew exactly who he was, made my heart soar. Watching them was like watching magic happen. He threw his arms around her neck and she wrapped an arm loosely around his little body. I thought I'd break down in the floor. The nurse took my hand and I looked at her, noticing tears at the rims of her eyes.

"They're saying if she has a home nurse, and continues therapy, she can leave soon," she commented. I smiled, but it quickly faded. With everything going on, I couldn't bring her back to my apartment. I couldn't expect Isaiah to take her in. I definitely couldn't expect Mr. Charles evil ass to put her up. Even if he did, I wouldn't even want her anywhere near those people.

"About how long are they talking?" I asked.

"A month maybe." I nodded. I needed to get some things situated, and fast.

We stayed with G-mama for about an hour. It was so refreshing to see her smile and listen to her talk. It was minimal, but still. I wanted so bad to ask her what else she remembered, but I was sure there were years of memories. I silently prayed we'd have years to catch up.

~~~

"Well?" I couldn't wait until I got Lil Rell to sleep to ask Isaiah how his meeting went.

"Well, she didn't know anything," he answered plainly.

"Bullshit!" I yelled at him.

"Honest, and you can ask my mama, I think he has her scared outta her mind. He's not gonna tell her where he stays. They always met up at hotels. He ran up on her a couple of times leaving out the house. The first time was to give her your key and have Theresa run up in the place. He gave her three days, and when nothin' happened, he caught her at the gas station and threatened Tamika."

"Who is Tamika?"

"The baby." I rolled my eyes. Up until that point, I hadn't even thought of the kid having a name. "She said she didn't go to the police because he claimed to have them in his pocket which is why he ain't been locked up yet for what he did to you." I contemplated that for a minute, then dismissed it. There was no way he had anybody in his pocket. The reason he wasn't locked up yet was because there was no evidence. The same reason I hadn't been locked up for beatin' the shit outta him.

"We gon' have to find some way to get to him. I still think she bullshittin'. I know I'd do anything to keep me and mine safe."

"I don't know, Lea. She seemed pretty shaken up."

"Anyway," I rolled my eyes at him. "I wanted to ask you something."

"I'm all ears."

"You know my G-mama is doin' better." He nodded. "Well, they say she may be able to come home in as early as a month. She definitely won't be in my apartment, and I don't wanna impose on you, so I was wondering if you wouldn't mind helping me look for a house... for us." He cocked his head to the side.

"*Us* as in, you, yo' granny and Lil Rell?"

"And you, I mean, if you wanna come." My heart was beating outta my chest and I prayed my facial expression didn't give away my indecisiveness. What the hell had I just done?! I hadn't thought about that. How the hell did it just fly outta my mouth like that? Was it my sub-conscious talking? I couldn't turn around and say *sike*! Not with him grinnin' and cheesin' at me the way he was. He scooped me up and carried me to his room, staring at me. He sat me down and undressed me, taking his time with everything, massaging me as he went. I smiled, enjoying being spoiled. He spun me around and bent down to kiss the back of my neck. His tongue slid down to my butt and he kissed the crease of my back as he slid his hand between my legs. His fingers were so thick and they were instantly wet as he moved them in and out of me and caressed my cheeks with his tongue.

"Bend over," he mumbled. I did as I was told, and he dug his tongue between my legs, making me shudder and my legs go weak. "Uh uh, stand up." I tried to keep my legs straight, but he was goin' to town like he hadn't eaten in days.

"Oh my God." I didn't wanna cum yet. It was happening way too fast, but he was determined. He sucked my lips like his life depended on it, and I gripped the sheets as the vibrations pulsed from my womanhood through my entire body. "Oh my God," I mumbled again and my legs went out, but he didn't give in. He licked and slurped until I was begging him to stop.

"Turn around." He was all business. His serious face was in full effect and those damn green eyes had gotten dark. He hoisted me up and I wrapped my legs around his waist. He cupped my butt and slid me onto him, slowly, teasing me. I held on for dear life and moaned as he filled me up. He slow-stroked me and I licked his neck. He threw in a hard thrust, moaning in my ear, and I bit his shoulder. He picked up the pace, showing me no mercy. I yelled and cursed in his ear, scratching his back as he drilled into me.

"I love you," he moaned into my neck.

"Oh shit...shit. I love you too," I gasped as I came again.

21

"I got news," Mesha blurted out. It was empty in Q'doba except for us and I glanced up at her from my naked burrito bowl. It was Terrell's birthday. Three weeks had passed since Mesha's place had been shot up and Derrick was still a free man. Needless to say, I wasn't in the best of moods at all. Mesha had asked me to lunch to get my mind off of things, but so far, she had been unsuccessful.

"Wassup?" I asked, uninterested.

"I found this out a couple days ago, but I waited until today to tell you." I perked up a little bit. "My realtor friend got back in touch wit' me and you and Isaiah got the house!" My jaw dropped. When Mesha said she had a realtor friend, I didn't even really pay her any attention, but with Derrick wreaking havoc on everybody and my G-mama needing a place to stay, I took her up on her offer. It was a nice two-story, three bedroom in Compton Heights with a guest house connected to it that was great for G-mama. It was so perfect that it was almost too good to be true. I had tried not to dwell on it the past couple of weeks. Isaiah and I had been looking at other places, but nothing caught our eye like that one.

"Are you serious?" I smiled at her.

"Yes, heffa! I begged and begged him to let me be the one to tell you if y'all got it, so you better be happy as hell."

"I'm more than happy as hell." I went over to her and squeezed her, kissing her cheek over and over again.

"Ok, girl stop kissin' on me. I told you I only did it that one time!"

"Shut up!" I laughed at her and sat down. It slowly sank in that I was getting a house with Isaiah. We'd be living together, with Lil Rell and my G-mama. I exhaled. It was one huge weight off of my shoulders, among plenty other ones.

"Guess what, though." I stuffed chicken and rice in my mouth and looked back up at Mesha, waiting. "I found a new place too." I almost choked on my food.

"Really?!" I smiled at her. "I didn't even know you were looking!"

"I was, but I wasn't."

"Where is it? Come on, gimme details!"

"It's in Frontenac."

"Frontenac?!" I almost spit my soda in her face. "How the hell you get a place in Frontenac?" I didn't wanna sound like I was better than her by any means, but I wasn't even looking anywhere near Frontenac. I was a city girl at heart.

"That's where my man stays," she commented, staring out the window.

"Excuse me?" I asked. "You ain't said a word about a man in months and, even if you had, which I don't remember, how is it that strong that you movin' in wit' him and I don't even know his name?" I felt a little salty. We didn't hide much of anything from each other, especially if it was that important.

"You know his name..."

"What?!" I yelled. "It's somebody I know and you ain't said nothin'?"

"He didn't want me to."

"Wait..." I put my fork down and scooted back a little bit. "You gon' have to come clean right damn now before I get a attitude."

"Ok, ok! We started talkin' on the phone a while ago, and we just clicked. He's busy working a lot so we spend as much time as we can together."

"I guess he does work a lot if he live in *Frontenac*. Who the hell is it?" She took a bite of her burrito and mumbled something and I crossed my arms. "What?" I asked with an attitude. She finished chewing and blew out air. I was about to slap her.

"It's Dr. Ashwin." I blinked...a few times.

"Mesha, are you doin' it wit' my doctor?"

"His name is Samir... and *hell* yea," she nodded.

"*Mesha*!" My mouth dropped. She stared at me, watching my reaction. "He *is* fine, though," I laughed.

"Oh my God, Lea I didn't know what you were gonna say!"

"When, heffa? And why the hell didn't you tell me? Forget what *he* say! And how y'all about to be livin' together? I got *all* the questions!"

"We started talkin' not too long after you got out of the hospital. Well, I started callin' him-"

"Thirsty ass-"

"Whatever, you admitted he was fine. But he agreed to take me out if I didn't say anything because he didn't make it a habit of dating women he met in the hospital. So we started goin' out whenever we could, then he started *makin'* time for me, I met him for lunch at the hospital a few times, spent the night at his place a few times, and oooh lemme tell you that bad boy is nice!"

"This girl snatched up a doctor!"

"I used to be a gold-digger, I did."

"Yes, Mesha, I know," I laughed.

"But Samir is smart, and funny, and *so* sweet. He listens to me, he doesn't judge me, and I told him a lot of stuff I probably shouldn't have." She shook her head. "He is *so* easy to talk to and he's open with me, and oh my God the sex!"

"It's good?" I chewed my food and stared at her intently.

"JaLea," she slapped the table with her palms and shook her head. "It- is- amazing! You know I'm a G, right? I normally have 'em runnin' away from *me*. I talked all shit to him day in and day out before we did it, and he barely said anything. I just assumed he wasn't all that and

I'd have to teach him what I like. Baby, he did some marvelous shit that I ain't *never* had done to me before."

"Spare me," I laughed. She ignored me and kept talking.

"I was outdone. And he always pull me in to lay on his chest and hold me when we finish." She lifted her head and let her eyes roll back. I just ate and smiled at her. "What?" she asked.

"It sounds like you really like him, boo."

"I do, JaLea. I really do. I felt so bad for keepin' it a secret, but after the shooting, he kept askin' me to come stay with him and it seemed like we were doin' more than just messin' around and I couldn't keep it a secret anymore." I nodded, dumbfounded. It seemed like my girl had finally found somebody who could tame her wild ass.

~~~

"When can we start moving in? Can I put my house up yet?" Isaiah was like a kid in a candy store. He jumped up and down and spun me around like I was Lil Rell.

"As soon as we sign all the paperwork." Isaiah yanked me to him and kissed me. "I'm so excited about this," I told him as I stared at his sexy, yellow ass. *My man.* "You doin' ok today?" He asked. I knew why he was asking. The fact that he remembered what the day was, and was sensitive to the idea that I might be feeling a little down, made him even more sexy.

"Yea, I'm doin' ok today." I kissed him, and as soon as I was reaching for his belt buckle, my phone rang.

"You gon' get that?" he asked.

"Hell naw." I undid the belt and let it clang to the hardwood floor. I slid my hand into his shorts and started to stroke him. Making him weak had me wet. The way he shivered when I touched him, the way he looked at me like he needed me all the time, it gave me a high. Then his phone started ringing. "Wow, really," I complained. I licked my thumb and rubbed the wetness across the tip, making him squeeze his eyes shut and cringe. I was determined to mess wit' him since he decided to answer anyway.

"Hey Mr. Washington," I let out a quiet laugh. Since I didn't answer, I guess Aaron decided to call Isaiah. I got ready to stoop down and see if he could handle my head and still keep up with the conversation, but he grabbed my wrist. I was about to curse him out until I looked at the expression on his face. "Ok, I will." I pulled my hand away and he shoved his phone back in his pocket.

"Wassup? What's wrong wit' him?" He exhaled before he spoke.

"Theresa committed suicide."

22

Me, Lil Rell, Isaiah, Kim, Mesha, and a few of my dad's friends from work were packed in his living room. Isaiah and I had stepped out to get some Popeye's once we saw that more people were coming. I could tell that we all just wanted to keep him upbeat. He was trying to put on a front, but I knew him. It took a minute, but I was able to pull him off to the side.

"How are you doin'?" I asked him.

"I'm doin'," he replied.

"That's not an answer. It's ok to be upset in front of me. I know you loved my mama, but I also know, in some sort of weird way, you loved Theresa too. It's ok to grieve." He wouldn't look at me. He kept his eyes trained on the floor. I felt for him. As far as I knew, he had only had two meaningful relationships, and he had lost both of them tragically. I couldn't help but think that Theresa wasn't handling Terrell's birthday well at all.

"Did you want me to get you a soda?" A woman walked up to us and I automatically got an attitude. Aaron must have felt it because he immediately stepped between us.

"Yes, please, a sprite." I watched until she walked away towards the kitchen, then looked back at him. He rolled his eyes a little and laughed.

"So, who is that who so nicely interrupting our conversation?" I asked with my arms crossed.

"That is my friend, Yvette."

"And is *Yvette* more than a friend?"

"Yes, *mother*, she is."

"Oh." I nodded, staring at her. She was pretty enough, slim, maybe late thirties. "How old is she?" I asked.

"She's 39, she works with me at the post office, we've been friends for a while, more than friends for only a couple of months which is why I hadn't said anything, she lives ten minutes away, she's Puerto Rican, divorced, two sons, 20 and 16, never been on drugs, yes she knows I have, and she doesn't judge me, as long as I stay clean, which I am, she's been very supportive, waiting to meet you, and she hates it has to be under these circumstances." I stared at him in disbelief and curled my lip up.

"Really dad?" I asked. He laughed.

"I know you, I know you're nosey, and I wanted to get it all out of the way before she got back," he blurted out. "Hey, Yvette." I spun around and there she was, grinning in my face. "I want you to meet my daughter, JaLea. JaLea, this is a very close friend of mine, Yvette." I held out my hand to shake it.

"It's nice to meet you, Yvette."

"It's so good to finally meet you too, JaLea." She smiled a pretty, genuine smile, causing me to warm to her a little. "I hate it had to be over tragedy like this."

"Me too. I don't know why he didn't introduce us sooner." I shot him a look. All the time I was hounding him and Kim and he had a woman anyway. I was happy for him, though. It had been a while since he and Theresa had been together, he was clean, had a job and an apartment, and now he had a woman. I smiled watching the two of them together. I tried to steal glances at Kim, wondering if she was watching them or if she seemed jealous at all. She was actually minding her own business, mingling and having conversation with some of my dad's friends.

We'd been there about an hour when there was a knock at the door. My dad went to answer and I saw Mr. Charles step through with Erica and the baby. I was surprised that he decided to bring his bougie ass to the slums with us common folk, and after our last run in when Isaiah had to put him out of my place, he wasn't high on my list of people to see. I wouldn't be ignorant though. I actually felt sorry for him. He had lost his parents, his grandson, and his daughter all within the last five years. I went and got Lil Rell from in front of the television and walked him over to Mr. Charles. When we locked eyes, there was no animosity, no anger or ill will. I simply handed him his great-grandson. He held on to him for dear life and let the tears flow freely down his face. The apartment was quiet as he grieved silently. Lil Rell kept his arms locked around his neck until he pulled him back.

"You ok, Pawpaw?" he asked in the sweetest voice, making Mr. Charles smile.

"I will be, son." He put him down and we both watched him run away. "May I have a few words with you?" he asked me. I looked at Mr. Charles in shock.

"Me?" I gestured towards my chest and he nodded. I looked around, like I needed somebody to watch my back. Erica was staring at us, and turned away quickly when I looked in her direction. She knew what was up. Isaiah was staring too. I shook my head to let him know I didn't need any backup. I wasn't up for any bullshit, and I'd be sure to tell Mr. Charles just that if he got out of line.

We went out on the porch and sat down, just the two of us. It was weird, us being in each other's presence and not arguing.

"Theresa came over to the house this morning. She was crying and very visibly upset. I assumed it was because it's Terrell's birthday. I tried to calm her down, but she was inconsolable, so I sent her upstairs to lay down." He paused. I could see the hurt and turmoil in his face. I wanted to urge him to go on, but I sat silently, waiting for him to continue whenever he was ready. "I should've gone up sooner-"

"No, Mr. Charles. Don't blame yourself." I started to rub his back, but decided against it. Instead, I kept my hand planted on the step beside me.

"I went up to check on her and she was..." he stopped mid-sentence. "Her eyes were open, but she wasn't there." He sobbed softly, and I wondered why he needed to talk to me. I felt like shit for not crying, but he knew I wouldn't be the most sympathetic person to cry to. I wasn't ignorant, but I felt more calm that Theresa's hurt and anguish was gone, and less hurt that she was no longer with the living and breathing. I couldn't bring myself to cry, only pray that she made it into Heaven with her grandparents and her son where there were no drugs to hinder her. "There was a letter on the desk next to the bed where I found her." He had peaked my interest. He went in his shirt pocket, pulled out a folded piece of paper, and handed it to me. "I hate for you to find out like this, but I needed to clarify some things with you." I took the letter from him, eager to find out what he could possibly be talking about.

My son was the best thing I ever done in my life and he took him from me. Everything else I did wasn't shit. I almost died when my baby died, but I had to be punished for things I did. Daddy I'm sorry I know I didn't make you proud. Please tell Jalea I'm sorry. I was jealous of her because Terrell loved her and I felt like he didn't love me. When Derrick started helping me I was so happy somebody was finally on my side. I wanted to get back at her for taking my baby from me and he wanted to get back at her for his brother. I loved Kyra no matter what anybody thinks. When he told me his brother killed her, I wanted to be mad, but I wanted somebody on my side. Somebody to understand me. I know now

that it was stupid. It was him. All this time
I was trying to get back at Jalea and the
little nigga who killed Terrell was right under my
nose. I saw him today. He told me
what he did. I thought he was lying at first.
He told me he killed my baby. He told
me he tried to kill Jalea. He told me he was
gone kill everybody because I messed up.
All I had to do was steal and I couldn't even do
that right. Maybe if I'm gone then I can
make up for helping him. Maybe if I'm gone I can
see Terrell again. Maybe if I'm gone everybody
can finally be free. I'm sorry Jalea for blaming you.
I knew you would never hurt my baby. You loved
him too much. I'm sorry daddy for disappointing
you. I'm sorry Aaron for stealing all those years
from you when you could've been happy
with some nice woman and all you had was me.
I'm sorry everybody. I love yall.

23

I read and reread Theresa's letter three times before I handed it back to Mr. Charles. I could feel the tears welling up in my eyes and, as hard as I tried to shake them off, they started falling anyway. I always wondered what would happen when Theresa found out that Derrick killed Terrell. I had even fantasized about being the one to break the news to her. I never assumed it would lead to suicide. I never thought that she had any regret in her soul at all for the way she treated me. I never thought she had a care in the world if it didn't have anything to do with shootin' up or tryin' to come between me and Terrell. Apparently, I was wrong. All her demons had caught up to her and, sadly, the only outcome she saw was suicide.

"I can't imagine how it must feel to find out what that boy did." Mr. Charles put his hand on my knee, attempting to comfort me from what he thought was brand new information.

"I already knew," I whispered. He slid away from me clean to the other side of the porch.

"Excuse me!" he yelled.

"No, it's not like that. I found out what was going on and went to confront him. That's how I ended up in the hospital." Mr. Charles rubbed his forehead.

"My God. It all makes sense." He continued to rub his forehead, softly at first, then harder, until it seemed like he was about to rub his skin off. I slowly grabbed his hand and held it in mine. The July heat was almost unbearable, but we sat outside, holding hands for a while, letting reality sink in.

~~~

"Can I talk to you?" I hadn't been back in the house for a good five minutes before Erica was in my face.

"You should be talkin' to me from behind somebody's bars," I snapped and walked away. I was headed towards the bathroom and Isaiah ran up behind me. "This is barely the time or place," I told him with an attitude.

"Really?" He folded his arms. "You got a dirty ass mind, you know that right?" I rolled my eyes. "I was coming to ask you why you won't talk to Erica."

"Because I don't want to talk to Erica."

"Why not? She obviously has another side of the story-"

"Why would I wanna hear it, though? She obviously needed to prove somethin' to me. The way she came at you when she was in labor, and her goin' behind my back fuckin' a dude I was fuckin'-"

"Please, spare me," he cut me off.

"I'm just sayin'. That's what she get, tryin' to one up me."

"She may have details she wouldn't give me or maybe she remembered something. You don't know what she has to say unless you talk to her." I glared up at him.

"Fine," I sneered, and turned to go to the bathroom. It was only a couple of minutes to myself to think, but I figured that maybe losing her aunt had shed light on some things. Plus, deep down I did want to hear what the bitch had to say.

"So wassup?" I walked up beside Erica just as she was packing up her baby to go. She jumped and looked at me. I laughed inside, knowing that I had scared her. It was a shame the dislike I had for her. Just the sight of her in my daddy's house made my ass itch.

"I just wanted to talk about a few things." I held my hands out, asking what it was she needed to talk to me about. "Can we go outside?" she asked. My shoulders slumped, but I went back out into the heat. When she joined me a few moments later and didn't have her baby, I couldn't help but hope that it wasn't Isaiah who was holding her. I shook the thought from my mind, ready for whatever she was about to say. "First off, I know you know that Derrick is Tamika's dad." I nodded. No news there. "I want you to know that it wasn't like I went behind your back or anything. I met him back when I first moved in wit' you and Terrell." She paused and I closed my eyes. Her mentioning his name while talking about Derrick did something hurtful to my soul. I wondered if the pain would hit me the same years down the line like it still did with my mama. "We kicked it and hooked up a few times. Nobody ever saw him 'cause it's not like he was my man or anything. But I still had a attitude wit' him when I brought him to Isaiah's party and he called you baby. We got into it that night after he took me home and I swear I think he put somethin' in my drink because the next thing I know, I woke up half naked on the couch and he was nowhere to be found."

"Yea, he's good for slippin' shit into drinks," I commented. She shook her head.

"So you know!" It looked like she was pleading to me. "I swear, JaLea, I wasn't on any bullshit or anything. I didn't hear from him again until after I had Tamika. I didn't even hear *about* him anymore until you came asking Uncle Charles about some money."

"Get to the good stuff." I was inclined to believe her, but she wasn't telling me anything I really cared about. I could care less how she ended up pregnant by that psychopath. I wanted to know why she pushed up on Isaiah and why she didn't call the police when Derrick threatened her.

"Me and Isaiah already had our fallin' out over the issue. I just didn't want to deal wit' that dude anymore, and I knew Isaiah was a good guy."

"That's why you tried to get him back when he was nice enough to sit wit'chu at the hospital?" I asked her.

"I was desperate," she admitted. To hear her admit something like that made me pause. "I never had anything like what you and Terrell had. And I always saw the way Isaiah looked at you. When I found out y'all were together, I got jealous. I never had anybody look at me like that and that's what I wanted. I'm sorry I went at him the way I did. It's not that I even want him, I just want the feeling of bein' wanted. I knew he wouldn't budge, I just felt the need to try." She looked down at the ground, and for a split second, I felt sorry for her. She deserved to be loved, not by Isaiah, but she did deserved happiness.

"Yea, Isaiah is great," I agreed with the driest voice I could muster up. Erica sucked her teeth like she was tired of puttin' on the apologetic act. I'd hate to fight on my daddy's porch after he had just lost his ex, but if she pushed me to it, it was gon' have to go down.

"After I had Tamika, I was at home alone, and Derrick just walks in like it was nothin'. I didn't know how he got a key, but he scared the shit outta me. He came right in my room, picked up Tamika and started singing to her. I just kept thinkin' about you, what he did to you, what you went through. I felt like I was about to throw up. He started rambling about you comin' back from the dead to try and kill him, payback is a bitch, he was still gon' get to you. He was holdin' my baby and all I could do was stare and pray he wouldn't do anything to her. He said he needed my help to get back at you. He gave me a key to your place and wanted me to go and break stuff and scare you, but I couldn't. Like two weeks later he came back. I was sleep and I woke up with him standin' over me. He said he could get to me and Tamika any time he wanted, and I saw how easy it was. He said if I didn't wanna do it then to have Theresa do it, and that if he had to wait much longer I'd wake up one day and Tamika would be gone and the police wouldn't be able to do anything." I watched Erica as she talked and she truly looked scared as shit. Her expression seemed like she wanted me to say something, to let her know I forgave her, or at least understood. I stayed quiet. "Look, JaLea, I'm not sayin' we need to hold hands and shit, but I'm tryin' to finally be completely truthful to you. It's fucked up it took my aunt dyin' to make me say somethin'." She stopped and took a couple of breaths to keep her cool. "But it is what it is. I tried to say forget it and not do what Derrick wanted, but when he threatened my daughter, shit got real. You'd choose Lil Rell over me without anybody havin' to ask, and I did the same. I apologize for the way I acted, and I really hate the way things went down. As much as we fought and argued, you still family and I love you and I'm happy that nigga didn't get what he wanted. Even though his ass is probably still somewhere plottin', you are still happy and healthy. You may be watchin' your back, but you're still here. I regret that I even let his ass in my life, but what's done is done and the only thing I can do is figure out how to move on for my daughter." She folded her arms, breathing heavy and I couldn't help but smile at her. "What?" she asked.

"That's the Erica I learned to know and hate." She cracked a smile and looked down at her feet. It would take me a while to get over her and Isaiah, but she was right. She was family, her and Mr. Charles. They irritated the shit outta me, but I wouldn't wanna see either of them hurt, just like when I heard about Theresa and my gut dropped into my feet. They were Lil Rell's people, so they were my people too.

"Can I ask you something?" I nodded at her. "I was scared to even ask Derrick what his issue was with you. When I asked Isaiah the other day, he told me to ask you." I nodded my head and braced myself, silently cursing Mr. Charles and Isaiah for leaving it up to me to fill in the blanks for her. How was I supposed to tell her that her baby daddy killed her cousin and pushed her aunt to suicide?

"Ok," I started. "Brace yourself."

24

"We get a new house today?" Lil Rell squealed.

"Yea we do, lil' man," Isaiah answered him. Watching them together almost made me forget about everything that was going on in our lives... almost... The moving truck was parked in front of the apartment and Isaiah, my dad and a couple of their friends from work had come over to help us move. I scanned up and down the street looking for cars I didn't recognize. The last thing I needed was to move to get away from Derrick just for him to be watching from somewhere anyway. It felt like the nigga constantly had me and all my people under surveilance. Isaiah had begged Kim to stay at a hotel for a minute until things died down.

"And what's a minute? When will things die down?" she asked him. "I'm stayin' right here in my house. I know how to shoot a gun," she had told him.

"Who is that?" my dad asked. Isaiah and I turned to see a slick, black Chevy pickup truck pull up behind the moving truck. We watched as Dr. Ashwin got out.

"You called your doctor to help us move?" Isaiah asked, sounding confused as hell. I laughed at him.

"Nope, she did." I gestured towards the car. Dr. Ashwin had walked to the passenger side and opened the door for Mesha.

"Oh you gotta be kidding me!" My dad started bugging up and Isaiah joined him. "Looks like she wore you down, young man," he said to him as they walked up on the porch. Dr. Ashwin laughed and nodded his head.

"That she did," he answered.

"Oh please, I didn't have to try as hard as y'all think." Mesha nudged him in the arm.

"Hey Dr. Ashwin." Isaiah held out his hand for him to shake.

"Hi, Isaiah. And please, you all can call me Samir."

"Hi, *Samir*," I teased. He turned and hugged me. "Take care of my friend," I whispered.

"Sure thing," he whispered back. "You're looking very healthy, JaLea," he commented once we pulled away.

"Thank you. I feel healthy."

"Ok, let's get this show on the road." Isaiah clapped and rubbed his hands together like he was really excited to do some work. Mesha and I loaded boxes as the guys moved the furniture.

"You and JaLea wanna take the truck and I can ride with one of the fellas?" Samir asked once we were all finished. I cocked my head at them.

"Ooh, I see you. Drivin' the truck, ok!" I teased them as I hopped in. "So how is in Frontenac, with Samir?" I asked once we were on the road.

"Biiitch, oh my God! I love that man."

"Girl, whatever."

"I'm for real." We stopped at a stop sign and I looked over at Mesha. She turned towards me with the most serious look on her face. "I have never been wit' anybody like him. He accepts me, he takes care of me, and not just financially 'cause I know that's what'chu thinkin'." She pointed at me and squinted her eyes, making me stick my tongue out at her. "Ooh and he cooks his ass off, Lea. I don't know what the hell I be eatin' half the time but oohwee! He is so smart. I mean, I know doctors have to be smart, but he's history smart, numbers smart, politics smart. He can have a conversation about anything, and that shit is so sexy. He ain't said it yet, but I'm pretty sure he loves me too. He wants me to go with him and meet his parents next month when he gets vacation."

"You say what?!" I was surprised things were moving so fast, but I was happy as hell for her. She deserved somebody who treated her like a queen.

"Yes, boo and they're excited to meet me. I'm stupid nervous, girl, I hope I don't get the bubble guts." I tried not to laugh at her, but I couldn't help it.

"Mesha, you are a nut."

"Man, I saw a picture of them and my jaw dropped. His mama is freakin' gorgeous, and his daddy look like who I'mma be fuckin' in twenty years." I turned my nose up.

"I'mma need you to not look at his dad like that."

"Wainch, you know what I mean. He looks just like his dad. They look so damn perfect, and then it's me. I'mma have to wear something conservative and concentrate extra hard not to curse."

"He likes you, loud, ghetto, and all. That's who he wants to meet his parents. I'm not sayin' you should wear coochie cutters and call his mama a bitch, I'm just sayin' be you. That's who he loves."

"I just don't wanna nut up," she responded. I nodded, thinking about how I felt when Isaiah and I told Kim we were together. I had known her for years and still yearned for her acceptance when it came to him.

"I understand. Theresa never accepted me and I even thought Kim had a problem wit' me and Isaiah at first, but what's important is how Samir feels. He wouldn't want you to meet his people unless he was serious about y'all. That says a lot. His parents will love you. And if they don't it doesn't matter because Samir loves you."

"Aww," Mesha grinned. "That was sweet friend, but if his mama don't like me, I'mma end up cursin' her out.

"Oh my God, Mesha!" I laughed.

It felt like it took hours to get everything in, even though Mesha and I only carried in a few boxes and let the men handle the rest. We were standing at the back of the truck laughing and joking, and I could've sworn I caught a glimpse of dreads out of the corner of my eye. I snapped my head in the direction I thought I saw him, but there was nothing. I was trippin'. I squinted and searched the tree-lined street. The sun was beaming down, there were a few kids out on bikes and running around, a couple of people gardening, a woman was out reading under the shade of her porch, but there was no sign of a deranged man with dreads. I turned and looked at my own house, the house I shared with Isaiah, and smiled, praying for a new beginning.

25

"She's a little down today." The receptionist stopped me at the desk as soon as I walked in. "We were thinking it was a set back until we realized what today was." I nodded at her. It was August 12th, eight years to the day since my mother had been killed. That was the reason I chose that day to take G-mama home. I was hoping we'd have something else to think about for the day. Isaiah and I had spent the past couple of weeks making sure her space was perfect, and we had found the best home nurse for her. I knew she'd protest, but I wasn't budging. She may have been well enough to come home, but it was with the understanding that a constant eye be on her at all times until she had passed all her physical therapy checkpoints. Even then, I'd probably keep the nurse on for a little longer, just until I was comfortable leaving her alone. Mr. Charles had been more than happy to switch the funds Terrell had left for her facility care to her home care, and I was thankful for that. Everything was in place.

"Hey G-mama," I tried to sound as cheerful as I could, but when she turned around with tears in her eyes, my bottom lip started shaking. I walked over to hug her and she stood up to greet me. I stopped in the middle of the floor. My hands flew up to my mouth and I swung around to the nurse.

"She wanted to surprise you," she shrugged her shoulders. I practically knocked my G-mama down when I ran over to hug her. I felt sixteen again in her arms.

G-mama leaving the facility was a bittersweet moment for everyone involved. The staff was more than happy with the way she had progressed over the last few months, and I promised that I'd bring her to visit them and the friends she had made. After what felt like a hundred goodbyes, we packed ourselves and her belongings in the car and pulled off. It was surreal, having her sitting next to me, riding home, to stay.

"Isaiah didn't come?" she asked and I laughed. "What?" I glanced at her, reminding myself that she had obviously heard and remembered everything I had said to her over the years. "I can't wait to finally meet him. I remember when Kim was pregnant with him. Her and yo' mama were real close." Listening to her was amazing, like hearing your kid speak their first full sentences. "I really wish I would've gotten to talk to Terrell. I really wanted to, every time he came with you, but..." She stopped and I looked at her. Her eyes glazed over and I reached for her hand. "I'm so sorry, baby. I wanted to talk to you, believe me. I never wanted to leave you. I wanted to be there for you." She shook her head and snatched her hand away from me.

"It's okay, G-mama. We both went through it. I understand-"

"No. It's not ok. I can't imagine what things were like for you to find out what Tasha did, find out who she really was. And when you had to go to the police station. I thanked God for Terrell and his family. I thank God they took you in. Except for that Theresa. I never did like her-"

"G-mama," I started.

"Nope, she was trifling then, and she's still-"

"G-mama!"

"What?!" she yelled.

"Theresa passed away." She huffed and grabbed her seatbelt. "Oh Lord! Forgive me. I do not speak ill of the dead. What happened?" she asked, I kept my eyes on the road as I told her about Theresa's death and the funeral. It had been overly awkward for me. People I hadn't seen in years, people I flat out didn't know even though they were my son's family. I still hadn't fully processed my thoughts for her, even as I watched them lower her into the ground. I loved her for giving birth to my first love, but I couldn't stand the things she did to me and my mama, or the way she treated me because I was with Terrell. I absolutely adored the way she was with her grandson, though. She doted on him as much as she possibly could. It was almost irritating, but I understood she was trying to make up for the time she had missed with Terrell. On the other hand, I couldn't stand her for being the one helping Derrick terrorize us. I shook my head. There were so many levels to how I felt about Theresa.

"So how do you feel coming home?" I asked, changing the subject.

"Oh, baby I feel like I'm gettin' outta jail. Not that they didn't treat me good, I'm just happy to be able to move around and come and go as I please."

"Where you tryin' to go, G-mama?"

"Hell, anywhere. Everywhere!" I started to laugh, but it was cut short when I glanced in the rearview mirror. Derrick was right behind us. I froze, scared as shit.

"Fuck," I mumbled under my breath.

"Hey, I'm the only one in the car who can say fuck." In any other situation, I would've been laughing, but my heart was racing against itself. I talked all big and I had all these ideas in my head of how I'd handle him whenever I came back in contact with him. I realized that was only if I planned it, if I was the one who was waiting for him and had him cornered like I had in the back of his apartment building. Knowing that he was following right behind us and that me and my G-mama were in danger at the very moment was pushing me into a panic attack. My chest got tight and it felt like my heart was about to explode. "The light is green." I heard G-mama, but I couldn't stop looking in the rearview mirror at his eyes, those eyes that had deceived me for months. Then he smiled. He knew that knew. He knew I had spotted him, and he got a kick out of it. I wanted to put my car in reverse and floor it clean into his ass. "JaLea, you ok?" G-mama asked.

"Yea, I'm good, sorry." I took off slowly and he followed behind me. A couple of cars pulled around, honking their horns as they zoomed past. I noticed an opening between traffic and made a quick left. Sure enough, he swooped left after me.

"JaLea, what the hell? I just got out the joint. You tryin' to send me back."

"It's good to see you still have a sense of humor," I joked between nervous breaths. I glared up into the mirror, but I couldn't see him good enough. I knew he wasn't above taking shots at people in the broad daylight, which was what had me the most nervous. "G-mama, can you grab my phone outta my purse please." She did like I asked. "Dial 9-1-1."

"What for? Why are you drivin' like a bat outta hell?" I huffed, practically running a stop sign. "You better start talkin', lil' girl."

"You remember Derrick I told you about."

"What kinda question is that?" Her voice was grave. I could only imagine the thoughts she had about him.

"He's behind us."

"You say what?!" She started to turn around.

"No!" I yelled at her. "Please," I added softly. She was fresh out of the facility, but I knew she'd still backhand me in a minute. She turned the phone over in her hand and fumbled with it. "How in God's name am I supposed to work this thing?" she asked with an attitude.

"Oh Lord," I mumbled and took it from her. I called the police and put them on speaker phone.

"9-1-1, what's your emergency?" the dispatcher came on.

"Yes ma'am, the emergency is there's a deranged lil' boy following me and my granddaughter. He tried to kill her a while back and now he's hot on our heels and ain't no tellin' what he might do!" I stared at her wide-eyed. "What, girl? Ain't that what's happenin'?" I shook my head.

"Where are you, and what are your names?" the dispatcher asked. I trained my eye on the rearview mirror as I made a quick right. Derrick followed. I rambled off information, irritated that he had a cover on his front plate. I swear his ass thought of everything. I wondered how often he had tailed me without my even knowing. I was desperately trying to figure out where I could ditch him. I definitely wasn't about to drive home and I wouldn't dare go to anybody else's house that I knew. Then it hit me and I smiled to myself.

"Come on bastard," I goaded.

"Yea, come on bastard," G-mama repeated. "Why do we want him to come on now?" she asked, confused.

"I'm goin' to the police station. It's not too far away on Jefferson," I told her. "Hopefully he's trippin more off gettin' to us than where we're goin'." After a couple of blocks, I hit Jefferson and turned.

"Did he turn?" G-mama asked.

"Yep," I smiled. The smile soon faded when he turned off Jefferson a block later. He was too doggone smart. It was stupid of me to think he wouldn't know where I was leading him. Always one damn step ahead.

26

"It was so nice to finally meet you face to face, Isaiah. So handsome and strong." I grinned and gave G-mama the side eye. "I'm positive you'll take such good care of me here in your home." She had been laying it on thick all through dinner. I'd rather hear her talk about that than our adventure on the way home. I had begged her to keep her mouth shut so that I could tell Isaiah what happened after dinner.

"Thank you so much Ms. Blasik," he replied.

"Oh please, you can call me G-mama. You shackin' up wit' my baby, might as well." I resisted the urge to groan out loud. She was a mess. I was so overjoyed to have her home and well again, but she was a mess! I waited until we had gotten G-mama and Lil Rell off to bed before I broke the news to Isaiah. As soon as I got it out, he started choking on his water.

"What do mean he was following y'all?!"

"Just that. I don't know when he ended up behind us, but I tried to make him follow us to the police station and he turned off Jefferson."

"Why didn't you call me?"

"I called the police, Isaiah. What were you gonna do?"

"Oh, that's nice, make me feel like I ain't doin' shit." I rolled my eyes.

"You know damn well that's not what I meant. At that point-"

"Baby, when shit like this happens, you don't wait hours to tell me. How do you know he didn't follow you home? We just got here. Your grandma is here now."

"He won't hurt her-"

"Oh, he won't?" Isaiah asked sarcastically. I turned away from him to start washing the dishes. "You don't even believe that yourself, JaLea." I kept my eyes on the running water, trying not to think about the fact that I had brought yet another person into my web of bullshit. G-mama had been much safer where she was.

~~~

"I figured you didn't know since you hadn't said anything." I sat across from Kim on her couch in shock. Lil Rell, clueless as to what was going on, ran around behind us screaming his ABC's.

"No, I didn't know." I stared at the blue spot on her tan carpet where I had wasted Kool-aid so many years ago. I remembered apologizing over and over again when I couldn't get it out, but she had made me feel so much better. She was so forgiving. I was just the opposite. Especially when it came to her sister. Hearing that Tasha was up for parole hit me somewhere so deep that I couldn't even figure out how to react. "I got a P.O. box when I started stayin' wit' Isaiah. I guess I need to go check it."

"Yea, she told me, but I got a letter too, so yours is probably in your box." It was silent, except for Lil Rell and his plane noises. I couldn't think straight. Was Kim gonna be by her side? Was she gonna speak on her behalf? Were they gonna try and bring up the fact that she had been assaulted? There were so many questions floating around in my head.

"Did you wanna say something else?" I asked her. It was starting to feel like I couldn't breathe.

"I wanted to talk about it, get your feelings on things, tell you mine."

"How about we start with yours, because I'm pretty sure you know mine," I told her.

"Well, I feel conflicted. I know you don't wanna hear this, but I love my sister. I do. I didn't bother you about the appeals over the past couple of years because I knew there was so much more on your mind." I looked at the front door so she wouldn't see me roll my eyes. "It's really hard though, for me to look past her faults and bad decisions. I wanna be there for her but what she did cost Kyra her life." It had been so long since I actually heard somebody speak my mama's name that I had to catch my breath. "I don't know how much time is sufficient enough for her to pay for that mistake, especially since she did practically the same thing to you." I nodded my head. Again, there were a number of things I wanted to say. If she did get out, she might end up on Derrick's shit list too since he assumed she snitched on him. I'd love to see him fuck her up. "JaLea?" Kim asked, concerned, like she could hear me.

"Oh, huh?"

"I asked how you feel?" she repeated. I had to think long and hard before I answered. I didn't wanna disrespect Kim, but she already knew I could care less about Tasha, so I really didn't know what she expected from me. I swallowed hard.

"Personally, I think she needs to rot in there. And if she does get out, I'mma make her life a livin' hell."

~~~

"You told her that?!" Isaiah yelled as we drove to Ted Drew's.

"Yea. What was I supposed to do? Lie? Yo' mama has always been able to catch my lies from miles away. Besides, what did she expect me to say?" Isaiah laughed as we climbed out of the car, He rushed to open the door behind him and help G-mama out. "I don't understand why you wouldn't sit in the front," I told her.

"Because I don't pay no bills. I'm perfectly fine to get out of the car by myself. I'm 58, not 85." I laughed as I closed my door and blew a kiss to Lil Rell. He had the cutest grin on his face while he gripped Isaiah's hand and skipped towards the line.

"My friend!" he yelled and pointed. I turned towards where he was pointing and spotted Derrick. Immediately, I turned back. Isaiah and G-mama were deep in conversation.

"Isaiah!" I screamed at him and he stopped dead in his tracks. I motioned across the street where Derrick still stood with a fuckin' grin on his face. Isaiah calmly put Lil Rell's hand in mine and kissed me on the forehead.

"Be right back, baby." My breath stopped at a lump in my throat. Terrell had kissed me and walked right into a gunfight. Isaiah kissed me and the same asshole who kept fuckin' me over was waiting for him too, smiling. I tried my hardest to breath, but my lungs wouldn't listen. I felt G-mama's hand rubbing my back.

"It'll be just fine, JaLea," she whispered, and I finally exhaled. Everything seemed to happen so fast after that. Isaiah walked clean up to Derrick and clocked him dead in his face. Derrick fell into the side of the building he was standing next to. I quickly picked Lil Rell up so that he wouldn't see as Isaiah swung over and over again. A group of onlookers started yelling and recording with their phones.

"Oh, he is beatin' his ass," G-mama smirked. I wanted to be happy, but anxiety was getting the best of me. The scary thing was that Derrick hadn't moved a muscle. He watched Isaiah walk over to him and didn't so much as flinch. He didn't even attempt to block or dodge the punches at all. He was struggling though. Or at least I thought that was what I was seeing, until I heard the gunshot.

"Oh God." I automatically dropped down to the ground as the spectators started to scream and scatter like roaches. I couldn't gather and process my thoughts right before G-mama was yanking at my collar. I glared at her and she was still staring across the street. I turned and saw that Isaiah and Derrick were goin' at it. I breathed a sigh of relief until I realized that they were fighting over the gun. I came to my senses and shuffled Lil Rell back to the car. The last thing I needed was for my son to be traumatized. I ran back to where I left G-mama standing just in time to see Derrick give Isaiah a quick push and run through the gangway. Isaiah tried to run after him but fell after a few steps. I hurried across the street to where he was laying. It felt like my head was about to explode as I stooped down to him.

"My side," he moaned. I reached over, feeling that his shirt was drenched. I couldn't move my hand. I knew it was blood, and I knew the sight of it would make me pass out.

"*Please*, Isaiah," I begged. "I'm so sorry. Please stay wit' me." He gave me a weak grin before he passed out.

27

"I can't deal wit' this. I'm a bad luck charm. I swear I'm fuckin' *bad* luck-"

"No such thing as a bad luck charm." Mesha followed me as I paced the waiting room.

"Then why the hell does this keep happening?! Why do I keep losing people?" I asked her.

"Everybody loses people, boo-"

"You need to stay out in Frontenac wit' Samir and y'all live happy away from me and my bullshit. I'mma take G-mama back-"

"Stop talkin' crazy!" Mesha grabbed my arms and yanked me around to face her. "Isaiah ain't dead so stop actin' like it. He's in surgery and it wasn't even life threatening."

"It didn't have to happen in the first place!" I yelled at her.

"Okay listen, you can't blame yo'self for what's goin' on no more than you can blame yo mama," she blurted out. I felt the tip of my mouth curl up in anger. "Don't look at me like that either. It's not yo' fault, it's not yo' mama's fault. It's that punk Chris fault and his stupid ass brother. Those are the people you need to blame. Not yo'self." I looked at her, then over at Kim who was sitting in the corner with her face in her hands.

"How much you wanna bet *she* blames me." I nodded in Kim's direction. She didn't speak to me at all when she got to the hospital. She had been in the corner the whole time. I wanted to approach her, but I was so scared of what she might say, that she'd lash out me. Before Mesha had a chance to answer, a man walked straight over to Kim and wrapped his arm around her shoulder. She looked up at him and when they embraced, I cocked my head to the side. I stared at his side profile, noticing he was damn near the spitting image Isaiah. Of all the years I had known them, all I ever heard of Isaiah's dad was that he wasn't in the picture. He was like a ghost. Neither of them had bad-mouthed him at all, they just flat out didn't talk about him.

"Girl-" Mesha was yanking my arm out of my socket.

"I see him." I whispered.

"Is it him?" she asked. "Where you think he been for years?"

"I don't know. They make it seem like he don't exist. It'll be real messed up if he stayed in St. Louis all this time."

"Kimberly Burns?" The doctor's voice made us all jump at attention. Kim went and stood right in front of him. The man I assumed was Isaiah's dad stood with his arm around her shoulders. I stood right behind them with Mesha's arm around mine. "Good news, the bullet didn't hit any major arteries. It was a through and through, and he came out of surgery with no complications at all." Kim grabbed the doctor into a hug and he smiled. I breathed a sigh of relief and turned to hug Mesha. Kim didn't even turn to glance at me as she walked off with the doctor to go see Isaiah. I knew it wasn't the time, but I needed to know what she was thinking. I still needed her approval. She was the closest thing to a mother I had after I lost my own, and I wouldn't be able to stand her bein' mad at me.

"You think she'll let you see him?" Mesha whispered. All I could do was watch them down the hallway. I wanted so bad to be with Isaiah that my chest was hurting. I had to take a step back and let Kim have time with her son. That's how I'd want it if it were Lil Rell.

Thirty minutes later, Kim and the mystery guy she was with came from up the hall, walked clean past me and Mesha, and kept walking.

"You might be right. She won't even look at you," Mesha whispered. I rolled my eyes at her.

"Like I didn't notice." I grabbed my bag and went to the desk so they could tell me where Isaiah was. I tried to keep myself from hyperventilating while the nurse led me down the hall. I was readying myself for the worse, blood and cords and tubes everywhere. I walked in and he was propped up flicking through television stations. "Isaiah?" I called to him.

"Oh, hey babe!" His eyes lit up and I exhaled. I ran over to him and flung myself onto him.

"Be careful, be careful," he winced and I let up a little, but not a lot. The sight of him made my heart jump. I was so relieved. "You can't get rid of me that easy," he joked. I didn't laugh.

"How are you feeling?" I asked instead.

"Like I been shot," he replied. I rolled my eyes at him.

"I'm bein' serious, Isaiah!" I yelled at him. "I'm tired of people gettin' hurt."

"I'm sorry. I'm sore, ok. I'm just tryin' to lighten the mood because I know you feel like it's your fault, but it's not.

"How can you-"

"JaLea," he cut me off. "It's not your fault, baby." He grabbed my hand and squeezed it, looking me in the eyes. I wanted to believe him, I really did.

"Your mama doesn't agree with you. And I assume your dad doesn't either." We stared at each other. I wasn't breaking.

"Yes, that was my pops." I folded my arms and tried not to roll my eyes.

"Does he live here?" I asked.

"Yea he does." If we had been at home, then I woulda been on his ass. "He's married, ok. He was married when my mom got pregnant, and he's still married. He has kids a lil' younger than me." My eyed got wide. I wanted to know so much more, but I knew I wasn't about to get any answers right then.

"You had siblings all this time? Why didn't you tell me any of this?"

"Because it was between me and my mama. And now I want it to stay between me and you." I nodded at him. "That includes big mouth Mesha."

"Mesha does not have-" He shot me a glance, cutting off the lie before I even finished it. I nodded again. "So, your mom didn't say anything about me when they came in?"

"No, surprisingly she was only concerned about me." I rolled my eyes at him. "Why do you keep bringin' that up?"

"Because she hasn't spoken to me at all. She won't even look at me."

"She's probably just shaken up. Give her a lil' space. She'll be fine." I nodded, only half believing him.

~~~

The police waited two days later, and right up until it was damn near time for Isiah to check out, to come and ask him questions. If I had a dollar for every time I had been questioned by police in my life, I could feed all the homeless in St. Louis. The smug looks on their faces always made me wanna smack them all. Every last one of them. I questioned why they were even there. It was apparent that Derrick could outsmart the entire police department. He'd done it so many times that it was ridiculous.

"Well, that was reassuring." Isaiah said once they left.

"Yea, a complete waste of time," I agreed with him.

"Hey you two." Kim scared the crap outta me, making me jump at the sound of her voice. I stared at her, not knowing what to say. "Can I see you for a minute?" she asked me. I think that scared me even more. I glanced at Isaiah before following Kim out to the hall. "I have to confess to you that, initially, I blamed you for Isaiah getting shot." No surprise there. "I almost had a panic attack when you called me. I was terrified, I was upset, I prayed every minute on my way here. I had some time to think though, and I realized it could just as easily had been me. I'm actually surprised Isaiah and I haven't been targeted yet." I cocked my head at her.

"What do you mean?" I asked.

"I was right there with you and Terrell. We put Chris away together, remember? I pointed him out just like you did, but the focus was always just on you. You have lost so much, and it's a shame because it's not like you're out here dealing drugs or flashing guns at people. You are just trying to live your life and take care of your son. And you just happened to have chosen my son to do that with. I can't fault you for anything." The crazy thing was, I had never thought about Kim being a target. Hell, I had never thought that I might've become a target. I had learned years ago that life was full of twists and turns.

"Thank you for comin' and talkin' to me, Kim. I knew you felt some kinda way and I was really hurt. I already blame myself for so much, I couldn't stand it if you blamed me too." She grabbed me and hugged me.

"Can I get in on that?" Isaiah asked, hobbling up to us. It felt so good to see him up and about. Despite what I or anybody else said, I wouldn't have been able to forgive myself if Isaiah had been hurt any worse.

28

I had to brace myself for the conversation I was about to have with Lil Rell. Isaiah had been home about a week and I wanted things to be back to normal, whatever that was, before I talked to my baby. He may have only been two, but he wasn't crazy, and it wasn't a coincidence that he called Derrick his "friend" and pointed him out in a crowd of people. He had had so many questions that day, why were his friend and Mr. Isaiah fighting? Why did his friend hurt Mr. Isaiah? There were so many things I wanted to say but couldn't, wanted to say but didn't. I had questions too, but I had to let things die down before I went to him. He was in G-mama's wing of the house sitting at her feet while she lounged watching the DIY network.

"Ooh, JaLea, it's so much stuff I can do. They made a vanity out of a lil' dresser and a coffee table out of an old bench!" I gave her a half grin. It was so good to see her coming around, but I had other things on my mind.

"Hey, baby," I stooped down next to Lil Rell.

"Hi, mommy." He didn't look up at me. He was too enthralled with his monster truck.

"I need to talk to you for a minute," I told him. G-mama turned the television off. She knew what was about to happen. We had talked about it, when would be the right time, when he wouldn't still be scared about what he had seen. "Let's put the toys away, ok." I stared at my little curly head baby as he pushed his trucks under the table and sat Indian-style. He stared at me, waiting. "Remember a while ago when we went to get ice cream but had to take Mr. Isaiah to the hospital instead?" He nodded. "Can you tell me about your friend you saw there?"

"He comes to my school."

"Oh, hell naw," G-mama yelled. I shot her a look and she crossed her arms. I was trying to stay calm to keep Lil Rell from being scared, and she wasn't makin' it easy.

"What does he do at your school?"

"Read books." My heart was about to explode. It would've been easier for me to handle Derrick poppin' up around the playground like a creeper, but he was actually *inside* my son's daycare. They allowed him to be around kids! My kid specifically. How the hell is this dude able to continue to hide in plain sight? I swallowed, making sure not to look at G-mama, before I went on.

"Mommy is gonna call and talk to your teacher because your friend is a bad man, ok. If you ever, ever see him again, I need you to run and scream as loud as you can. Run to a teacher, me, Mr. Isaiah, G-mama, any adult you trust who can get you away from him."

"Why is he a bad man?" It was such an innocent question with such a complex answer. *He had stalked me, murdered your dad, vandalized our property on numerous occasions, extorted money from me, tried to kill me, pushed your granny to an overdose, shot up auntie Mesha's apartment, and now he's stalking you.*

"Well, baby some people don't want us to be happy or be able to be together. We don't like or have time for anybody who doesn't want us to be happy. Those people are mean and we shouldn't be their friends." I was looking him right in his eyes, trying to get his little mind to hear me. "You understand?" I asked. He nodded, even though he probably didn't right then. I didn't care how many times I had to reiterate it to him, but I'd make him get the point.

~~~

I couldn't wait until Monday to get to the daycare. I had still been sending my son there after he called Derrick his friend, not even letting the thought cross my mind that that's where he knew Derrick from. I had left him with Kim that day. She and Isaiah were skeptical about me handling it, since I hadn't given them any details on what I was planning on doing. Truth be told, I wasn't even sure myself. Even as I marched in the doors and up to Jamie at the front desk, I was winging it.

"Hey Ja-"

"Who is this?" I cut her off, practically shoving my phone and a picture of Derrick in her face. She slid back in her seat, looking like she wanted to fight. I didn't care. I needed answers.

"That's a parent here." I turned the phone back to look at it myself, like I possibly showed her something wrong."

"This man," I pointed to his picture. "He has a *child* here?"

"Yes. What's wrong?" My head was spinning. Derrick had a kid, besides the one he had with Erica? How could that be? He hadn't mentioned it... I laughed to myself. He hadn't mentioned that his brother killed my mama either. Why would he give me any real, personal information? "JaLea, what's wrong?" she asked again.

"Which one is it?"

"Huh?"

"Which child is his?" I asked. She shook her head, not wanting to say anything.

"I really don't want to be in the middle of anything. You're scaring me and I don't want any of the kids to get hurt."

"You think I'd hurt any of these kids, Jamie? Really?"

"I don't know what's going on, JaLea. You come in here acting all crazy, and you want me to give you personal parent information?"

"It's either that or I sit up here all day and tell everybody how y'all let a psychopath in here!"

"Look-"

"No *you* look. I'm not tryin' to go off on you, I'm not blaming you for anything. All I want is to know which kid is his. I'm not gonna hurt anybody, especially a child. That's not me. But I have some business I need to take care of, and if you don't help me then I definitely won't hesitate to act a fool." Jamie and I had a staring contest. I wasn't breaking my concentration. Finally, she blinked at me and shook her head. She got up and I followed her into Lil Rell's class. She looked around a few seconds until she found her, a pretty, chocolate little girl, around the same age as Lil Rell, with dreads pulled up into a ponytail. She was playing with a couple of other kids, laughing and jumping around. She seemed so happy.

"Is that all?" Jamie asked with an attitude. I sneered at her.

"What's her name?" I asked.

"Dee," she answered dryly.

"Does she stay all day?"

"She normally leaves at 2," she said with even less enthusiasm.

"Thanks." I gave Jamie a half smile, dismissing her. I watched Dee for a little, wondering how someone so beautiful could come from such a hateful person. Had he lied and seduced her mother like he had done me and Erica? It didn't seem possible that anyone who honestly and truly *knew* who he was would willingly have gotten pregnant by him. It could very well be that her mama was just as twisted as her daddy was. Had she known what was going on the whole time? Was she in cahoots with him? I had so many questions as I went out to my car. Looking at my watch, I noted that it was just after noon. I had less than two hours to kill. That would be a piece of cake. I had camped outside of Derrick's apartment longer than that on plenty of occasions.

    I decided to run and grab something to eat just to pass a few minutes. I was back by one. I made it a point to park out of plain sight though, just in case Jamie's ass felt like she needed to call somebody on me. The last thing I needed was police asking me why I was staking out the daycare. The minutes passed in no time and at a quarter 'til, I saw a few of people start to file into the building. I watched as a couple kids were escorted out by their parents. Finally, Dee walked out with a woman. She looked to be in her late twenties, brown-skinned, professionally dressed in a suit jacket, pencil skirt, and heels with her hair pinned up. She pushed her glasses back as Dee tugged on her arm, skipping to the car. They looked so overly happy. There was absolutely no way this woman knew the truth about her baby daddy. She loaded Dee into her Focus and I turned my car on to follow them. My heart was in overdrive the full fifteen minutes I was tailing her. When she pulled into her driveway, I parked and quickly hopped out of the car. I figured I had to stop her before she got in the house, just in case Derrick was there. I couldn't chance knocking on the door. Hell, I was already putting myself in danger just being there.

    "Excuse me!" I called. I caught her just as she was pulling Dee out of her seat. She took one look at me in my sweat pants, jacket, and baseball hat, scooted Dee back in, and closed the car door. "I'm sorry. Please forgive me for following you."

"Can I help you?" she asked. I took my phone out and showed her the picture of Derrick. Her expression turned cold. I couldn't fully read it, but that wasn't the look of happiness.

"You know this man?" I asked. She squinted her eyes and pursed her lips.

"Who are you?" she demanded. I wasn't thinking straight. I had a lead on Derrick, something I had never had before, and I let it cloud my mind. Instead of thinking of all the possibilities of who this woman might be, I just started running my mouth.

"My name is JaLea Washington. This man has been terrorizing me and my family for the last couple of years." The words came out before I could even think about what I was gonna say. I breathed in and out so loud I was sure Dee could hear me in the car. "I'm trying to find him before anybody else I love gets hurt." I kept the phone in her face, silently begging her to help me. I looked her dead in her eyes and I saw her face soften. Her shoulders slumped and she exhaled, looking down at feet.

"He's been terrorizing me and my family too."

29

I followed the woman, Kia, to a park a couple of miles away. She didn't want to be seen with me on her front, and I have to say I agreed. She let Dee out to run around and I sat quietly, waiting for her to start talking whenever she was ready. I was positive her story wasn't anything like mine, but I was extremely curious nonetheless.

"I met Terrell-"

"Terrell!?" I yelled at her. What the hell?!

"What?!" Kia yelled back at me.

"His name is *not* Terrell!"

"Well that's what he said, so excuse the hell outta me!" I had to check myself. I was yelling at her like she had done something to me when she was actually doing me a favor.

"I'm sorry," I apologized. "Terrell was my ex fiance's name."

"Ok?" she replied, obviously confused. "I can't say I'm even surprised he lied. What's his name?"

"Honestly," I laughed, "I'm not even sure. He told me it was Derrick, then he told me it was Anthony." I stared at her as she shook her head, clearly upset. "So he's not your daughter's father?" I asked her.

"Oh God, no! I met him like four months ago at White Castle." She looked out at Dee on the playground. "We started talking and he got overly protective, way too clingy, way too in my business for us to have only been talking the couple of weeks that we had been. I broke it off and at first, I thought he accepted it. Then he showed up at my place one day, scared me half to death. I had never even told him the area I stay in. He was talkin' crazy like he needed me, I was part of his plan, he wasn't gonna let me get away. I tried to shut him down easy because it was evident that he was a lil' crazy. Then a couple of weeks later, he showed up outside my daughter's daycare. He wanted to be put on the list of emergency contacts," she laughed. I'm thinking what the hell for. I waved him off and he grabbed my arm. He threatened me, and my baby, told me he could find out where my family stays just as easy as he found out where I stay." She huffed and shook her head. "I didn't believe him. I shrugged it off until all my parent's car tires got slashed. All eight tires. I went to the police, but I didn't have any evidence at all, there wasn't anybody that looked like him with his name in their database, which makes sense now, seeing as though his name isn't even

Terrell." He showed up at the daycare again and I told him I reported him. He laughed, dead in my face, and damn near yanked me into the daycare. I didn't wanna make a scene because of the kids. I didn't know what he would do, I didn't even understand what the hell was so important that he used me just to get on the visitor list at the daycare."

"My son," I answered her. She stopped and looked at me. I smiled at her, not knowing what else to do. "I was engaged to my son's father when he was murdered. His name was Terrell." I closed my eyes, trying to keep the tears at bay. "The man who told you that his name is Terrell, is the one who killed him." Kia gasped and her hands flew to her mouth.

"Oh my God, I'm so sorry." I shook my head.

"It's ok. It's been almost two years now. I'm taking it day by day." She stared out at Dee again, playing with a couple of other kids on the slide. I told her about my mama, Chris, and Tasha, and the twisted way that my mama's childhood boyfriend had completely fucked up my life. She listened, dumbfounded, and had tears in her eyes by the time I finished.

"I don't even know what to say," she commented. "It's amazing you are as level-headed as you are." I laughed.

"I wouldn't call it level-headed. I have my moments, like stalking my son's daycare waiting for you." She nodded in agreeance.

"Well that's understandable. But I can assure you that whatever his name is, he's not my daughter's dad. I'll tell the front desk that, I'll go to the police station with you and tell them what I know, whatever you need. And I am so sorry that I helped him get to your son. I had no idea-"

"It's completely fine, Kia. You were protecting you and yours. Besides, you tried to do the right thing and it didn't work. I don't blame you for anything."

Kia and I exchanged numbers and she guaranteed me that she'd do anything she could to help end the madness that had been going on. I went back and forth in my head about what I had done. I couldn't say that I had put her in the middle because she was already in it, but I silently prayed that Derrick's sneaky ass hadn't been watching her or her house. There was no telling who he was working with now, or how he was moving. He had me and everybody else paranoid. We all drove the same cars, worked at the same places, and had routines that anybody paying close attention could catch on to. I wasn't gonna go out and get a new car or job, and I didn't expect Isaiah, or Kim, or anybody else to. Mesha's lucky ass had moved all the way out in the boondocks with her doctor boyfriend. I wasn't tryin' to make that move. I was a city girl at heart. I had already let Derrick run me out of one place. I wasn't about to uproot my baby and my man. Plus, now I'd be uprooting my G-mama too. Something needed to be done about him. He was a ghost though. That was the problem.

~~~

"Thank you for watchin' him," I said to Kim once I got to her house. I stared at him at the kitchen table eating. It was amazing how much was going on in his life and he wasn't even aware of it. That was my job though, to shield him from the bull crap.

"You know it's no problem," she replied. We hadn't really talked since Isaiah had gotten out of the hospital, and I missed her conversations. I got her up to speed about the events of the day and all she could do was shake her head.

"It's really beyond frustrating that nothing has been done about him yet. And now he's involving people that have nothing to even do with us at all." I nodded, agreeing with her.

"I been wantin' to ask you something," I started, unable to keep my mouth shut. I had promised Isaiah I wouldn't say anything and I wasn't gonna tell her what he told me, I was just curious as to what she was gonna say. "Isaiah always told me he didn't know who his dad was, but the man at the hospital looked just him." Kim turned away from me towards the kitchen sink even though there were no dishes. When she turned back around, there was a pained look on her face.

"Yes, that was Isaac, Isaiah's father." She wrung her hands together. "They see each other every blue moon, but that man has a wife and a family."

"But what about when Isaiah was born-"

"He was off limits then, and he's off limits now," she cut me off. "And that's all I'm gonna say about that." I shut my mouth. If that was all she had to say, then I wasn't about to push the issue. "I did need to talk to you about something else though." We left Lil Rell in the kitchen and settled on the couch. "Tasha was granted parole," she said. It was like a quick gut punch. I knew I heard her right, I just couldn't respond right then. "JaLea?" Kim leaned a little in my face as I stared at the living room table.

"When is she getting out?" I asked.

"Next week." I could feel the depression setting in. "She doesn't have anywhere to go so she was approved to stay here until she can get on her feet." I knew she was up for parole, but I hadn't let myself believe that she'd actually get out. She'd only served a little over half of her ten-year sentence. I definitely hadn't expected her to be staying with Kim if she did. It made sense though. She was her sister. I was just the kid of a friend who had passed away. I popped my knuckles and hopped up off the couch. "JaLea!" Kim yelled. "Stop for a minute." She grabbed my arms. "I want you to sit down, calm down, and process this." I wanted to snatch away from her, grab Lil Rell and walk clean out. "I'm having this conversation with you because I love you and I consider you family. I want you to always feel welcome here." I turned to face her.

"How do you expect me to step foot in this house while she's here?" I asked. "You want us to hold hands and have sing-alongs?" I stormed into the kitchen to put Lil Rell's jacket on.

"Oh don't be dramatic, JaLea! She's my sister and you're like my daughter. I'm not saying the two of you have to get along, but she's gonna be a part of my life and I don't want you to drop off the face of the earth because of it. Especially now that you and Isaiah are together." I wasn't sure what she expected from me. I wasn't her. My heart wasn't anywhere near as big as hers. I'd dealt with way too much bullshit. I scooped Lil Rell up and walked right past Kim to the front door where I paused.

"I have to think about it."

30

"Next week, huh?" Isaiah rubbed my back while I laid on his chest. I closed my eyes, letting his strong heart beat soothe me. "That's crazy."

"How does it feel?" I asked him.

"How does what feel?"

"You're about to meet your aunt for the first time."

"I don't know that woman," he laughed. "I should be askin' you how *you* feel."

"Like I wanna fight her ass. I was eight seconds off of yo' mama-"

"Come on now, baby, don't fight my mama," he laughed.

"You right, she's too *dainty*," I joked. He gave my hair a tug and I punched his chest.

"Yea alright, my mama got a good four inches on you. I bet she can wear you out."

"Boy, *you* can't even wear me out."

"Is that right?" he asked, sliding his hand down the back of my underwear. I turned my lip up at him. "I said," he cupped my butt cheek. "Is that right?" I grabbed his dick through his boxers.

"I can play too, and better than you." I smiled at him and he nodded.

"Bet." Before I knew it, he had flipped me on my back.

"That ain't fair. You can't use your strength."

"Oh I'm about to use *everything*." I tried to play fight with him, but he was all business. He yanked my shirt up and gripped my chest, sucking my nipples, making me arch my back to him. He slid my panties down while he kissed his way to my belly button. I was already wet when he slid two fingers in, slowly, teasing me. I grinded on his hand as he brushed his lips past my panty line. He blew his cool breath on my pearl tongue and I lifted my butt to meet his mouth. His tongue was so hot on my lips. First it was long, slow licks, then he sped up, dipping it in and out of me. I grabbed my pillow and shoved it in my face to keep from screaming out loud. It wasn't long before I felt the shock waves rippling through my body. He shoved his hands under my butt and held me in place while I came so I couldn't scoot away from him.

"Shit! Ok, ok! I can't-" He had me begging. That tongue was something else, but what I really wanted was that monster in his pants. He sat up with a smug look on his face. "Oh, you think you did somethin'?" I asked him. He cocked his head at me.

"Oh ok." He dipped his head back down and I slid clean back to the headboard.

"I'm playin'!" I yelled. I couldn't take any more. I couldn't stand him because he knew it. He stood up on the bed and dropped his boxers, making my mouth water. That yellow thing stood at attention, ready for action. I circled my tongue around the head and slid him in slowly, grinning inside when he moaned. I moved him in and out, slurping until he yanked away. "Can't take it?" I asked him, licking my lips.

"Keep talkin' shit," he smiled. "I got you." He threw my legs on his shoulders and dug into me like there was no tomorrow. He made sure he kept me climbing the walls.

~~~

I woke up with a jolt and the hairs on my arms were standing straight up. I looked at the clock. It read 3:13 a.m. I could've sworn I heard a noise. I sat as still as I could and strained to hear. After a few seconds, there it was again. It sounded like something scratching against the floor. I shook Isaiah.

"Wake up," I whispered. He groaned, turning away from me, and I shook him again. "Isaiah," I whispered a little louder.

"I'm sorry, baby, I can't again," he complained.

"No, boy. I heard a noise."

"It's probably just G-mama movin' around."

"She's in a whole separate part of the house, Isaiah. We woulda heard her or the nurse through the monitor anyway." It happened again and he shot up in bed right beside me. It was like furniture being pulled across the floor.

"What the fuck?" Isaiah yanked the covers off of him and slid back into his boxers and t-shirt. He grabbed the bat from the side of the bed and I hopped up to follow him through the hallway. "I hate you don't want me to get a gun," he mumbled.

"In here wit' Lil Rell? No sir." I gripped the back of his t-shirt, taking baby steps behind him as he walked.

"You think I'd leave it somewhere he can get to it?"

"I wish you'd focus," I told him as we crept closer to the stairs. We paused at the top, waiting to hear the noise again. After a few seconds, he started down with me on his heels. My chest started throbbing right where my scar was. I knew it was just in my head, as it always was. The only part of me that was left from that night was that scar on my chest. It was like an alarm that went off in my body when I felt like Derrick was near me. My heart was beating so fast that it was getting hard to breathe. The anticipation was killing me. We crept quietly step by step. When Isaiah hit a creaky one, all hell broke loose. There was clearly someone running through the house downstairs. Isaiah took off chasing the noise and I followed. I was about to pass G-mama's space when her door flew open.

"What the hell is goin' on?!" she yelled. I stopped dead in my tracks when I saw her with a bat.

"G-mama! Where did you get that?"

"My grandson-in-law gave it to me," she bragged. I sneered at Isaiah as he walked towards us with the bat stretched across his shoulders.

"Whoever it was got away," he growled.

"What do you mean 'whoever it was'? We all know who it was!" I yelled.

"Who was it?" G-mama's nurse asked, walking up rubbing her eyes. "What happened?" I rolled my eyes at her. Isaiah stormed off to the office to look at the camera footage. G-mama, the nurse, and I were right behind him. He clicked on the security television and I watched, growing more and more pissed off, as every camera was knocked out. I felt sick to my stomach.

"Are you fuckin' kiddin' me?!" Isaiah threw the remote against the wall making the rest of us jump. "How the hell did he get in without the alarm goin' off?"

"Because it's Derrick, that's why." I rushed past everyone and ran up the steps. Tears were threatening to fall, but I refused to cry. I was so pissed off. This shit was beyond ridiculous. He had found me *again*. But of course it wouldn't be life if he hadn't. Hell, he knew where everybody else was, maybe except for Mesha.

"Mommy?" Lil Rell appeared in the doorway. I held my arms out to him and brought him in for a hug. He was my safe place.

"I called the police," I heard Isaiah say. I kept my eyes closed, concentrating on Lil Rell. He was everything my world wasn't. He was my calm during the storm.

"I ain't old, but I'm not about to climb these steps!" I heard my G-mama yell. "One of y'all need to talk to this nurse because she on the verge of quittin'!" I rolled my eyes. Weak ass. As much as my family had been through and she wanted to run away because of a break in?! I had to check myself though. She'd probably grown up with both parents, never seen any pain or experienced and hardship. Whatever.

"If she wanna leave, let her leave," I yelled.

"You say what?" G-mama yelled right back.

"You aren't thinkin' straight right now." Isaiah sat beside me on the bed. I kissed Lil Rell on the forehead and laid him on the bed behind me. "It took long enough to find her and I know you don't want G-mama here alone."

"G-mama don't even act like anything is wrong with her-"

"The home said at least until-"

"Fine, Isaiah!" I cut him off. I was overly irritated. "Will you talk to her then, because I don't have the patience right now." I stared straight ahead and he leaned over and kissed me on the cheek before heading downstairs. I almost let it irk me, how sweet and understanding he was. Derrick had found us! He'd been in the house! Knocked the cameras clean off the walls, and rigged the damn security system! He should've been pissed right along with me. I looked at Lil Rell who had fallen right back to sleep. I rubbed his back, shaking my head. All this bullshit was really ridiculous. I felt like I'd never be able to hide anywhere.

31

Pulling up to the Sanders' house brought back so many memories, from one end of the spectrum to the other. Although I hadn't been there in months, nothing had changed. It was still the same place where my life with my first love had started and ended. It was my son's first home, and, also, where his grandmother took her life. The holidays and arguments in that house swam through my mind, threatening to bring tears to my eyes. I put my feelings in check, walked up on the porch, and started banging on the door. After a few seconds, Erica swung the door open. I could tell she had a huge attitude that softened a little bit when she saw me.

"Hey, JaLea. What's wrong?" she asked.

"You tell me," I responded about ready to knock her head off her shoulders. "Have you seen Derrick lately?" I asked her.

"No, not since before... Aunt Theresa..."

"Are you bullshittin' me? Because I'll find out if you bullshittin' me."

"I don't even know what this is about!" she yelled.

"Guess who paid me, Isaiah, Lil Rell and my G-mama a visit in the wee hours of this morning!"

"Derrick?"

"Ding, ding, ding!" I clapped in her face.

"What the hell, JaLea? You think I'd come to you and rat myself out just to do the same damn thing? How smart is that?"

"How smart is it bein' on my bad side?"

"Like it ain't somewhere I'm used to bein'?" Erica shook her head at me.

"I don't put anything past you. Not one damn thing."

"Well that's yo' fault. I thought we were tryin' to get back on good terms, but you would rather believe the whole world is against you, and it's only Derrick. I didn't have anything to do wit' him showin' up at your house. *Nothin'*! I played my part in his lil' game already." I rolled my eyes, not wanting Erica to think that for even a second that she had gotten through to me. Maybe I *was* grasping at straws. I hadn't even let Isaiah know where I was going or what I was thinking. It was one of those snap judgements that I was so famous for. Sometimes I was right, but sometimes I was wrong. It did make sense that Derrick had just flat out found me, or followed me. I thought back to the day we moved in when I thought I saw him on my street. He was there, then he was gone. I figured my mind was playing tricks on me, but then again, maybe it hadn't been. Maybe his slick ass was always just a hop, skip and a jump away, watching my every move.

~~~

"I gotta visit you more often!" I told Mesha, walking into her foyer. The place was beautiful, even from the outside. It definitely gave the Sanders' house a run for their money. It wasn't as big, but it was luxurious and sexy. I was barely able to tell her about my conversation with Erica.

"Well you know what my answer is," she said after I finally finished. I half ignored her as I admired the living room. It was definitely still a bachelor pad, but Samir had good taste. The dark wood and black furniture complimented each other perfectly. The only real color in the room was the beautiful pictures. Indian art decorated the walls and I was in awe. Leave it to Mesha to ruin the moment. "I still wanna jump her ass."

"Why, Mesha?"

"What'chu mean why? Did you forget about Isaiah? Did you forget about Theresa, God rest her soul? Did you forget about her sucker punchin' you on *yo'* birthday?"

"Ok, Mesha!" I plopped onto the leather couch. "She said she didn't have anything to do with it, and I believe her."

"Yea, I guess. So, do you really believe that chick from the daycare?"

"Why wouldn't I?"

"Is it a coincidence that y'all been at the new place two months, but right after you meet wit' her, all of a sudden he pops up?" I sat thinking.

"Now that you mention it, it does sound fishy, but why would she lie-"

"To get you to trust her, *duh*."

"Ok, but wouldn't it be stupid for him to come to the house *right* after I meet her? He couldn't have waited a week? Don't it seem like *too much* of a coincidence?"

"Aye, if the shoe fit."

"Oh, how did I forget to tell you!" I almost scared Mesha. "Tasha is getting' out in a few days!" She frowned at me and rolled her eyes.

"What the hell for?" she asked with an attitude. "Don't she got like 18 more years or somethin' stupid like that?"

"She has less than five, but still. She didn't have to do all ten, and I always knew she could get out sooner with good behavior and all that other bull crap. I just never thought she actually *would*."

"So, are we beatin' *her* ass?" Mesha asked. I glared at her.

"I'mma pray for you."

~~~

I left Mesha's house in deep thought. It could be completely possible that Kia have been lying through her teeth and actually working with Derrick. I didn't know her from a can of paint. Why would she form an alliance with me? Could she have been the one who sent him to my house? Did she turn right around after I left the park and let him know I was checking up on moves he was making? I started my car and thought back to what Erica had said: *You would rather believe the whole world is against you and it's only Derrick.* I shook my head, irritated. Since when did Erica start making sense?! I pulled off, dreading the days ahead. Derrick knew where I lived and how to get in my house, Tasha was getting out of prison, I didn't know where me and Kim's relationship would be when she did, and if my relationship was strained with Kim, what would that do to me and Isaiah's relationship? We seemed strong right then, but there was never any telling what would happen from day to day. That was life. I had to get it off my chest though. I pulled out my phone and called my man.

"Hey, baby. Did you like the house?"

"It was beautiful, just like I thought it would be," I told him.

"What's wrong?" he asked.

"How do you know somethin' is wrong?"

"Because you ain't all like *oooh* Isaiah, it was soooo nice! It had this, and this, and that-"

"I don't sound like that," I laughed. "Anyway, I did wanna talk to you about something that's been on my mind."

"I'm listenin'." The calmness in his voice made me smile, but I was nervous as hell about what I was about to say.

"You know Tasha is getting' out in a couple of days and she's stayin' with Kim."

"Mmmhmm."

"I don't know how my relationship wit' Kim is gonna be after she gets out. I know how much yo' mama means to you. What if me and her can't get along?"

"Why wouldn't y'all get along?" He sounded so confused and innocent he almost reminded me of Lil Rell.

"What do you mean? Because Tasha is moving back!"

"So, you want her to choose between her sister and you, or y'all can't be friends?"

"Why are you makin' a joke out of this?" I felt myself getting' hot.

"Why are you takin' it out on my mama?" he asked.

"See, this is what I was talkin' about. She ain't even out and we're arguing already!"

"JaLea, I need you to put yourself in my mama's position and think about what's goin' on-"

"You don't know what it feels like to lose somebody like I did! You don't know how it feels! What happened to my mama was Tasha's fault! Why would I wanna look at her every time I go over there?"

"I know how it feels to sit beside your bed for almost two months wit' my heart breakin' every day. It was like a sick fuckin' dream that I couldn't wake up from-"

"And that was partly Tasha's fault too!" There was a pause on the other end.

"I'm not sayin' don't be mad at Tasha. All I'm sayin' is that my mama was there for you when nobody else was. You know it's not in her heart or mind to hurt you, so don't punish her for who she's related to. Tasha is her sister and she doesn't have anywhere else to go." I held the phone, thinking, getting pissed. I absolutely could not *stand* feelin' silly. He was right, though. The closest person I had to a sibling was Mesha. If she ever did some stupid shit, I can see myself havin' her back through everything, and I hadn't even grown up with her.

"You're right," I finally answered.

"I'm sorry, what?" he joked.

"You heard me," I laughed a little. It took a lot for me to admit defeat, and he knew that. We got off the phone on a good note. There was one person I still had to have a conversation with, and I was dreading it with every bone in my body. How was I gonna tell my G-mama that the woman who set her daughter up was about to get out of prison?

32

"At some point in yo' life, you gotta learn how to forgive baby." I sat on G-mama's couch with my mouth hanging open. She wasn't bothered at all by the news.

"But she's the reason-"

"Yes, you told me what happened. People do stupid things all the time."

"They don't always lead to somebody dying though, G-mama. How can you not be frustrated at all?"

"I didn't say that, I'm just not flippin' all out like you are. She did what she did. It was a terrible decision and we all paid a price for it. In the end, God will judge her, but that's not our business." I leaned back, defeated, drumming my fingers on my thigh. I looked at my G-mama, who really wasn't old enough to be a 25-year-old's grandmother in the first place, and I smiled. I knew she was ready to be independent, but it wasn't like she depended on us anyway. She had her own wing off the side of the house with a living room, kitchenette, bathroom, and an office space where the nurse slept. We could get to her wing from a door off the living room, but she also had her own door that lead outside to a patio where she'd go and relax. If she was persistent enough, I'd think about letting the nurse go. I hadn't expected for a minute for my G-mama to have a relapse, but the thought of Tasha being free was playin' with my head.

"I'm just worried about you," I told her.

"JaLea," she got up to sit beside me and put her hand over mines. "I need you to try and understand something that's hard for me to put into words. When I was... sick, I was still aware of everything that was goin' on around me. I could hear, I could see, I could remember, but my heart wouldn't let me respond. It might not make sense, but I wanted to move, I wanted to speak, I just... I couldn't." I sat there and looked at her, trying not to let the tears fall. I understood exactly what she was talking about. After Terrell's funeral, I was a zombie. Isaiah had cleaned me up and changed my clothes and everything, and I didn't say a word. I didn't even look at him. I was completely present, but I wasn't *there*.

"It makes perfect sense," I told her. I leaned in for a hug, trying to figure out how I could be as understanding as everybody around me.

~~~

Isaiah was cooking chicken alfredo for dinner. G-mama had insisted on letting her and Lil Rell help, so they were all in the kitchen, leaving me to some peace and quiet. I was soaking in a much needed, hot bath with a glass of Pink Moscato. I lifted my hand and let the suds slip down my arm as I watched, trying to clear my mind of everything. It wasn't working at all. Life swirled itself around and around my thoughts like the bubbles in the water. I shook my head, thinking about the book I could write about my life. Of course, there was always someone who was worse off, but my mind was still spinning thinking about all of my own bullshit. My phone vibrated, breaking my trance. I glanced at it, half expecting to ignore whoever was on the other end, but it was Kia. I groaned. *More bullshit*. After talking to Mesha the other day, I wasn't even sure how I felt about anything that Kia had told me about Derrick. I was scared and borderline desperate which had me doin' stuff out of the ordinary. Normally, I'd question anything anybody said to me, especially somebody like Kia who I had never met in my life. Yet I found myself caught up in her sob story.

"Hello?" I answered.

"Hi, JaLea." She sounded dry as hell. "I heard from Terrell."

"Really?!" I yelled in her ear.

"Oh damn, I'm sorry!" she apologized. "You called him..."

"*Derrick*," I corrected her, more irritated than I was before I answered the phone. I wondered how she could've forgotten what I told her about Terrell? The answer hit me quickly. Because it wasn't her life. "What did he have to say?"

"He said he had something big coming up in a couple of days and that he'd need me. I asked him what he wanted me to do and if it had anything to do with my daughter-"

"He said a couple of days?" I asked. My heart started pounding. Tasha was getting out in a couple of days.

"Yea. He told me not to worry about it and just be ready when he calls." My thoughts were in overdrive. What the hell was he planning and what was Tasha's role in it all? I wanted to scream! I wanted to call Kim and rat Tasha out and tell her not to let her move in. I wanted to call Kia out on her seemingly innocent act to see if she was part of the plan. There was so much I wanted to say that I just went blank. "Hello?" I heard Kia ask. "JaLea?" I sat, quietly. "Do you know something? Are my daughter and I in danger?"

"Y'all were in danger the moment he looked at you."

~~~

Isaiah and I met Mesha, Samir, and my dad at Denny's for breakfast the next morning. I I wanted to get everybody together sooner than later. Tasha would be a free woman in a little more than 24 hours and we needed to have some type of plan if the shit was about to hit the fan. G-mama had talked me into leaving Lil Rell with her and the nurse instead of taking him to Kim's. I hadn't even thought twice about inviting Kim. I didn't wanna put her in the middle of me and Tasha any more than I already had.

"So how much do you believe this chick?" Mesha, always the devil's advocate, spoke up first.

"I'm with her," Aaron commented. "Where did she come from? He randomly picked a woman from the daycare that happened to think he was nice lookin' enough to date, and she was foolish enough to lie for him so he can be around her kid, my grandson, and whoever else kids go to the daycare? Did she seem that dumb?"

"She really didn't," I laughed. "I admit, it sounds fishy, but it's too much of a coincidence that she called me talkin' about something that's goin' down around the same time that Tasha is supposed to be gettin' out."

"She's right, y'all," Isaiah chimed in. "We need to figure out how to protect ourselves and each other since the police aren't interested in doin' it."

"Y'all know I love my baby," Mesha rubbed Samir's arm, "But the reason I had to move wit' him was because my shit got shot up. So we need to be on our *Derrick* shit. Get sneaky, get conniving, or get illegal, so we can either dodge his ass, or catch his ass."

"I know I'm the newcomer here, but can I make suggestion?" Samir asked. "I have a security friend at the hospital who does a little moonlighting. He may be looking for some work if you all want him to spend a couple of nights outside of the house."

"That would be cool, Samir! Does he have any other friends that wouldn't mind doin' some moonlighting? I wouldn't feel right of we just took care of us."

"I can check," he answered.

"Well why he ain't been at *our* house?" Mesha snapped.

"We're good, babe. I got you." Samir put his arm around Mesha. She smiled up in his face and we all groaned.

"Y'all irk. I'm tryin to be serious." Mesha flicked me off without taking her eyes off Samir. *"Anyway,"* I laughed. "Samir, that would be a great idea. Thank you, because we know those cameras are about to cost us an arm and leg to replace." We all sat around for the next hour or so throwing ideas out there, trying to figure out a schedule to check up on each other until we figured out what was what. When we finally left, I felt like we were all on the same unsuccessful page. We all had smiles on our faces, but nothing had been accomplished at all. I felt helpless. What the hell were we supposed to do without knowing where Derrick was, or even where to begin looking? Samir's friend couldn't protect us all. I thought about telling Kia to text me when she saw him next, but that may be too late, or I could be walking into a trap. I shook my head as we got in the car. Isaiah grabbed my hand after turning the key.

"It'll be ok, baby. It has to be," he tried to reassure me. I kissed the back of his hand. I wanted so bad to believe him, I just didn't know how.

~~~

"Are you sure about this?" I asked Isaiah. He had packed Lil Rell a bag and sent him to Kim's so we could get away for what he jokingly called my last night of freedom. I didn't find it very amusing.

"Yep, I'm positive. Tasha gets out tomorrow and you are way too stressed out. I need to calm you down a lil' bit." He rubbed the back of my neck and moved his hand down to my chest and squeezed. "Big, juicy. That's what I'mma call you from now on."

"Big juicy?" I frowned, giving him the side eye. "How about you stick to 'babe.' I'm good wit' that."

"I promise I'll only say it when they in my face, hopefully in about-" he glanced at his watch. "Twenty-two minutes." I laughed as he pulled into the lot of the Hilton. "It's just on the second floor, let's take the stairs," Isaiah suggested once we checked in. I followed him to the stairwell and as soon as we were behind the door, he was on me. He yanked me up and pinned me against the wall, wrapping my legs around his waist. His face was in my neck, caressing it with his tongue. He pulled my shirt up and dug his face into my chest, giving me chills. "Can I take one out?" he asked.

"Do what you want. They're yours." I answered. He yanked a bra cup down and grabbed my nipple between his lips, making me moan. He swirled his tongue in circles and slid his hand down the back of my jeans.

"I don't wanna wait 'til we get upstairs," he mumbled. "I want you now." I didn't protest. He lowered my feet to the floor and wasted no time pulling my jeans and panties off. He kissed my stomach and slid his way back up until his face met mine. He kissed me, slow at first, then with so much passion it almost felt like the first time we kissed. I tugged at his belt until I got it undone, and when his pants fell, he stooped to lift me up. I wrapped my arms around his neck and moaned as he lowered me onto him. He filled me up and my eyes rolled back. I shuddered at the feeling, the warm, thickness of him. He rested his hands under my butt so he could control me, moving in and out with pleasure and ease. I bit into his shoulder as he dug into me with no mercy. The thought of somebody possibly walking through the door and catching us gave me an adrenaline rush and I tightened my grip and thrust back at him. "I love you so much, baby." I just barely heard him through the moans echoing off the walls. I smiled and bit my bottom lip.

"I love you too."

After we had finished acting like teenagers in the stairwell, Isaiah took me up to the room for round two. He was hungry for me and it felt damn good. Afterwards, he was out cold. I stared at him as he slept, even snoring a little. He was so sexy wit' his yellow ass. I traced his eyebrows, grinning at him, feeling silly. My phone rang making me jump and jolting him out of his sleep. I turned around to the night stand and snatched it up, noticing it was the nurse. It was after midnight and my heart sped up a little. Isaiah was right on my back as I said a quick prayer and accepted the call. I knew in my soul that it wasn't good news.

"Hello?" I asked, almost scared.

"JaLea!" the nurse yelled.

"What happened!?" I yelled back, my eyes immediately filling with tears.

"Y'all need to come home *now*! Yo' granny just shot somebody!"

33

"Faster!" I yelled at Isaiah as he sped through the streets, trying to get home.

"I'm driving as fast as I can, baby." I was in panic mode. The nurse said a loud noise woke her up and, when she ran into the living room, a man was lying in the middle of the floor and G-mama had a gun. Trying to talk to either of them was a chore. G-mama was in shock and the nurse was yelling so loud it was hard to understand most of what she said. When I asked if the man had dreads though, I heard her say no clear as day. I felt selfish as hell for being upset that he didn't. I needed to be worried about my G-mama and how she would be holding up.

"Damnit, I *knew* we shoulda got those cameras fixed as soon as we could!"

"It's only been a couple of days-"

"I don't care!" I yelled at the top of my lungs. Isaiah didn't say anything else. I felt bad for yelling at him, but at that point, I was just trying not to break down. Who the hell was in my house? Had Derrick recruited somebody else to do his dirty work again? It was too much of a coincidence that somebody *else* was trying to break in. The guilt of leaving was eating away at me. I couldn't wait to get to my G-mama, hug her, and make sure she was ok. I prayed the police had made it there and the two of them weren't just sitting in the house with the body. Sure enough, we pulled up and there were four police cars, a fire truck, and the coroner van. I shook my head. Three different neighborhoods, all disrupted by me. I hopped out with Isaiah right behind me.

"Excuse me, ma'am," an officer stuck his hand out to stop us.

"I'm JaLea Washington, this is Isaiah Burns, this is our house and my grandmother and her nurse are inside." I was out of breath and panicked. He looked us up and down and moved his arm for us to pass. We ran up to the door and stopped dead in our tracks. The room was crawling with police officers. There were two women stooped down where the body was in the middle of the floor. The man was sprawled out on his stomach and the scene made me think of Theresa passed out under my living room table. G-mama was sitting on her couch. The nurse was on one side with her arm around her and an officer was on the other side talking to her. She had a dazed look in her eyes that scared the hell outta me. I had seen it before, way too often. I grabbed Isaiah's hand

and squeezed, afraid to move a muscle, terrified that my G-mama was gone again.

"JaLea!" she yelled all of a sudden. I breathed a sigh of relief as she ran to me. "I had to. I had to do it." Her hands were shaking and I grabbed them.

"I know. It's okay." We hugged and I felt Isaiah's arms around us. I gave God a silent thank you. My G-mama was still with me.

"JaLea Washington?" the officer who had been on the couch had walked up to us. I nodded. She looked past me. "Isaiah Burns?"

"Yes," he answered.

"You two are the homeowners?"

"Yes," I replied impatiently and she finally glanced at her pad.

"Ok, apparently around midnight, Ms. Blasik heard noise in the front room. She grabbed her gun, and came out to check on things and caught the intruder," she motioned towards the body on the floor, "in the middle of a break-in. At which point she says she yelled at him to leave the house. He lunged towards her and she fired twice, killing him.

"Do you know who it is?" I asked the officer.

"There was no identification, no wallet, nothing but the clothes on his back. They'll take fingerprints at the morgue," she answered. I nodded and moved towards the body. Isaiah tried to follow me, but I shook my head at him. I needed to see who it was. I needed to look at his face and find out whether my nightmare was over. Derrick could've sent another poor dumbass in like he had done with Theresa, or he could have simply cut his dreads off. The women who were studying him looked up at me like I didn't belong.

"This is one of the homeowners. We need to figure out if she knows the intruder," the officer said. One woman moved out of the way so that I could stoop down and get a good look. My heart was pounding the closer I got, wondering if we could be just that lucky. "Isaiah!" Yelling his name was the first thing I thought to do when I looked at him. Even as they stared out into nothingness, Derrick's eyes still made my scar throb.

"It's him, baby?" Isaiah ran over to me and stooped down beside me. Surprisingly, he broke out laughing hysterically. I looked at him, then around the room where everyone had stopped their conversations to stare. It took a few seconds for it to sink in. When it did, I started laughing too. G-mama followed suit. I knew no one understood but us. It wasn't funny, not in the least bit. It was relief laughter. We had all gone so long with having to peek over our shoulders and watch our backs because there was no telling where Derrick would be. I laughed until I cried, and I cried until my ribs hurt. I cried for my mama, my G-mama, Terrell, my baby, Theresa, myself, Isaiah, hell I even cried for Erika and Kia. Eventually, Isaiah was able to calm me down as we piled G-mama and the nurse in the car to go to the police station. I wanted to believe the nightmare was over, but I still had Tasha to deal with.

~~~

Day was breaking by the time we made it back home. G-mama's nurse didn't waste any time packing her things and leaving. I didn't blame her. I didn't even try to explain to her that more than likely nothing like that would ever happen again.

"I don't need a nurse anyway, JaLea," G-mama tried to convince me. "What I need is a maid or a cook. Can that old man pay for that?" I laughed to myself, thinking about Mr. Charles's reaction to paying for a maid.

"I'm gonna have you sleep in the guest room until we get your place cleaned," I told her.

"Yea I figured that," she commented, plopping on the couch. Isaiah and I glanced at each other, knowing we had to have a conversation with her. The only thing they told me was that the prints taken from the man my G-mama had killed matched Anthony Merritt. Thanks... I already knew that. It pissed me off that he'd been in the system the whole time, yet, hadn't been caught. Even when I put him right in their faces, they had let him go. I had to try not to go off on everybody because my G-mama shouldn't have been in that position. He should've been locked up way before it even had to come to that.

I couldn't wait to get home and really get down to it. I needed to talk to G-mama away from the police. Those damn officers wouldn't let us watch while they were questioning her and they were treating her like she had done something wrong. It had me way too pissed off. It was so tiring going over and over the same story, trying to get them to realize that every day they couldn't find him, they had played a part in the horror story that had been my life. I sat down beside G-mama, and Isaiah sat on the loveseat across from us.

"G-mama, where did you get the gun?" I asked quietly. She looked from me to Isaiah, then down at her hands, then back up at Isaiah.

"Don't look at me!" he blurted. "I gave you a *bat!*" I stared at her, waiting for her to come clean. I didn't wanna push her, after all, she *had* just been through an extremely traumatic experience. But the wait was gettin' to me. After a couple of minutes, she finally started talking.

"A man came by the other day, said he was a friend of the family."

"A random man came by?" I asked with an attitude.

"Yes, he just showed up one day, said he knew y'all and that he had something for me."

"And you let him in?" Isaiah blurted out. G-mama rolled her eyes and huffed.

"Yes," she answered.

"What aren't you tellin' us, G-mama? This doesn't make any sense at all." Before she could answer, Isaiah jumped up.

"Wassup?" I asked, following him.

"If it was a few days ago, then the cameras were still up," he answered. I heard G-mama groan as she followed us. "When was it?" he asked, pulling up the camera recordings. She stood tight-lipped.

"G-mama?!" I yelled at her. She still didn't budge. "So, you're gonna make him go through every day looking for somebody walking up to your door when you can just tell us what day it was? How old are you again?"

"Who are you talking to, lil' girl?" she snapped at me. I had to check myself. I was trippin', but she was irritating me. We stared at each other, both beyond tired.

"I'm sorry," I admitted. She nodded in acceptance and crossed her arms.

"It was Thursday," she told Isaiah. He didn't waste time pulling up the date. The cameras automatically started recording whenever they detected motion. We never really checked the one outside G-mama's door because it was always her or the nurse. There were a few recordings for Thursday and we watched each one until we got to 1:34 p.m. Isaiah clicked play and my mouth dropped. He rewound it back a few seconds then paused it where the face was clear as day. He and I turned our heads at the same time to look at G-mama questioningly. When she didn't say anything, Isaiah turned his full body around in the chair to stare at her.

"My *dad* gave you a *gun*?!"

34

I stared at the image for what felt like forever. It was clearly Isaiah's dad. He walked up and knocked. G-mama answered the door and let him in after a few seconds. The video of him leaving was recorded eight minutes later.

"G-mama?" I shook my head at her. "Please explain."

"Yes, *please*." Isaiah followed. She shook her head.

"I forgot about the damn cameras," she muttered. "Y'all were never supposed to know where I got it."

"Yea, I figured that," Isaiah said with an attitude. "What did the police say about it?"

"They asked who's it was. I said it was mine. They left it at that." I shook my head at her answer.

"What did my dad say? What did y'all talk about? How do you even know him?"

"We didn't say much–"

"Oh, come on, G-mama," I cut her off. "He was here for eight minutes. You know how much can be said in eight minutes?"

"I wanna hear it from your mouth before I confront him. I need to know what's goin' on." Isaiah was practically begging. I felt sorry for him. On top of being confused as hell, the father he barely saw, and that I had never met, pops up out of the blue at our house, with a gun nonetheless.

"G-mama," I said after her silence.

"Ok!" She left the room to go back to the couch and we fell in line behind her.

"He already knew what was goin' on from Kim. After you got shot, he started digging, tryin' to figure out what he could about Derrick, but he came up with nothing." I rolled my eyes.

"Because his name isn't *Derrick*!" I yelled.

"Hey, I'm just tellin' you like it was told to me!" she yelled back. "He got wind that somethin' was about to go down and told me to protect my family." Isaiah and I stared at her.

"That's it?" Isaiah barked.

"That's it," she replied. I laughed a little. "What?" she asked defensively.

"That's not it. You're tellin' half of the story." I didn't wanna argue with her. Trying to pry and pull a story out of her when I was already drained of all energy was daunting. All three of us were yawning and G-mama was making me feel like I was talking to my son.

"It's cool." Isaiah clicked the computer off and got up. "We gotta go get Lil Rell from my mom's before she goes to get Tasha anyway. I nodded and we left G-mama sitting right there on the couch. Once we made it to our room, Isaiah sat on the edge of the bed and put his head in his hands. "I know my mama won't be up for another couple hours." He pulled out his phone. "My pops might be up." I grabbed his hand.

"I don't think this should be a phone conversation." He glared at me. "I know you need answers, but you also need sleep. We got a couple hours before we need to get Lil Rell. Let's get some rest, go get him, then call your dad." I felt selfish for being mad at that moment that I had never met the man before. I had only seen him in passing, but apparently, Isaiah had a lifeline to him and had been lying about it. And now the man had been to my house and corrupted my G-mama. I needed to be there to look in his eyes myself and know why. How does he know my G-mama? Why did he go to such lengths? And how the hell did *he* know something was about to go down?

~~~

"You nervous?" Isaiah asked his mama as I zipped Lil Rell's coat. I tried not to dwell on where Kim was headed. I tried to keep my mind focused on the fact that Kim had always been there for me, and I prayed that would never change.

"Very nervous," Kim answered, as she pulled on her shoes. I could see the strained look on Isaiah's face and I knew it was killing him to keep his mouth shut about his dad. We had agreed that it was best to tell his mama later, especially since it was in the back of our minds that Tasha may still have been in cahoots with Derrick. "I hope we can meet on common ground, JaLea," she said to me. "Maybe one day you'll even wanna hear what she has to say." I gave her a fake smile. Little did she know, I was dying to know what she had to say.

    Isaiah couldn't wait until we got in the car to call his dad. He must've called six times back to back before slamming the phone on the dashboard. I glanced over at him once I made it to a stop sign.

    "Calm down, baby."

    "Why isn't he answering the phone?!" he yelled.

    "I don't know, Isaiah. Maybe he left G-mama his number and she got to him before you did and told him what happened. Maybe he's asleep or working."

    "Bullshit! If she did call him then he definitely knows what's goin' on. All the more reason to answer my call!" He dialed again and hung right back up. "I just wanna know what he had to do wit' it. It's irritating the hell outta me that I don't know what's goin' on in my own house." I nodded, understanding him completely. I looked in my mirror and saw that Lil Rell was staring out the window. I prayed my baby was safe, that I didn't have to worry about what would happen to him or my G-mama when Tasha got out.

    "Maybe you should have your mom call him over when she gets back wit' Tasha and we can all talk. We can get to the bottom of this and find out what, if anything, Tasha has to do with it." I wondered if Isaiah was thinking the same way I was, though. There was no way Tasha wasn't in the middle of everything. I could feel it in my bones. I just needed to see it on her face.

~~~

"You want me to go wit' y'all? You know I got hands for days!" Mesha was always amped. No matter what was said, she found a way to get riled up.

"No girl! I'm not gonna fight her."

"Are you sure? You don't know what's gon' come outta yo' mouth when you get in her face." I sat quietly, staring at the television but not paying attention. Mesha was right. I had so much hate built up towards Tasha that I was liable to swing without even realizing what I was doing.

"Ok, Mesha, I'mma *try* not to beat her ass."

"Dang, you gon' end up hittin' her dead in her face! And I can't even come?"

"Girl," I laughed. "Isaiah is coming," I whispered, rushing off the phone.

"I just talked to my mama," he said as he leaned against the doorway. "So it's set. She's gonna have my pops meet her over there and we're all gonna talk about this."

"You didn't tell her what was up, did you?" I asked.

"I told her we had somethin' serious to discuss. She said she told him the same thing."

"Your dad has to know wassup," I replied. "What other reason would he be ignoring your calls? I wonder if he'll really show up."

"I don't know, but my mama said she'll be home in like forty-five minutes." I stared at him. *Forty-five minutes.* I couldn't get my feelings together. I couldn't for the life of me figure out how I was supposed to have a civilized conversation with Tasha and not curse her out or swing on her? I nodded about half an hour later when Isaiah asked if I was ready, even though I wasn't sure I could ever be ready to see Tasha outside of prison walls.

We rode in silence, Isaiah, Lil Rell and I. There was nothing that could be said that would ease the tension. Isaiah was eager to see his dad and hear his side of the story. I was focused on keeping my composure and getting answers to my questions. By the time we pulled up, Kim was already parked in the driveway. As I stepped out of the car, my heart started beating so hard and fast that I was almost in tears. I was scared I was about to have a full-blown panic attack, until Isaiah came up behind me and rubbed my back. The feel of his hand through my jacket was enough to calm me. Lil Rell grabbed my hand and took a deep breath as we walked up to the door. Of course, Kim was all smiles when she answered, like she didn't think for a minute that there were gonna be any problems at all.

"Hey you guys!" she beamed. I put on a fake smile, for her benefit, remembering that she had expressed her reservations about Tasha coming home also.

"Hey, mama." Isaiah sounded so dry as he hugged her. I followed peeking around the living room, not seeing Tasha anywhere.

"She's in the bathroom," Kim said, reading my mind. As soon as she said it, I heard the toilet flush. I felt my throat closing up, my heart was racing again, my hands began to itch like I needed to punch something.

Then I saw her. She rounded the corner from the hallway and stopped when she spotted me. Her face was stoic. I met her gaze with my own expressionless stare. I'd be damned if she saw how out of it I was. It was deathly quiet in the living room. Kim and Isaiah looked from me to Tasha.

"Mommy who is that?" Lil Rell asked, easing the tension. I looked down at him and smiled.

"That's..." I was stuck. What the hell was I supposed to say?

"That's my aunt," Isaiah stepped in. Lil Rell looked at me and I nodded. Before I knew it, he ran over to her and grabbed her leg for a hug. Out of instinct I tried to lunge and grab him, but Isaiah stopped me.

"Just let it go for now," he whispered. He held his arm around my waist as Tasha bent down and rubbed my son's arm.

"Hi!" she smiled at him. "You must be Terrell Jr."

"Yes, it is!" Kim told her.

"You are a cutie pie." She stooped down to hug him and I could've sworn I tasted throw up in the back of my throat.

"Why are you making me do this?" I whispered to Isaiah.

"Let him be innocent. He's a kid and he likes to hug."

"But her?"

"I'm glad you came, JaLea," I heard Tasha say. I looked at her and tried to find some hint of sarcasm. An inkling that she was bullshittin'. I didn't see any.

"Yea, we have a few things to talk about," I replied. There was a knock at the door that almost made me jump.

"That must be Isaac," Kim muttered. I felt Isaiah tense up beside me, knowing that his dad was there. I couldn't help but think that the shit was about to hit the fan. Kim opened the door and Tasha rushed past her.

"Hey brother!" she yelled, wrapping her arms around his neck.

35

"Hey, Tasha," Isaac mumbled. I cocked my head at them. Tasha was grinning and holding on for dear life, but Isaiah's dad had a pained look on his face. It was weird as hell.

"*Brother*?" Isaiah asked.

"That's your dad, right?" Isaiah stayed still, eyes fixed on is father. "Well then," she smiled. I looked over at Kim who was acting completely oblivious.

"How about I take Lil Rell into the den and we can all sit and talk," she said. Then she disappeared with my baby, leaving us all staring at each other.

"Why didn't you answer my phone calls?" Isaiah blurted out. His dad started shaking his head. "What? You had to know what was up when I was callin' you like crazy. But you answered for my mama, huh?"

"Don't talk to your dad like that," Tasha had the nerve to jump in.

"What?!" I yelled at her. "Who are you to talk to Isaiah like that?"

"Can we all just calm down a little?" Kim asked jogging back into the room. Tasha, Isaiah and I started speaking all at once, trying to plead our case like siblings to our mother.

"Hey!" Isaac yelled. "We're not getting anything accomplished like this." He and Kim sat beside each other on the love seat and we all followed. Isaiah and I sat on the couch and Tasha sat on the lounge chair. "Now that we've all calmed down, we all know why we're here, so I have something to say."

"Is it gonna be the truth? Because if not-"

"I have no reason to lie right now," he cut Isaiah off. "Your mom confided in me about what was going on after you were shot. I started digging around and heard that this guy was planning on trying to get into your house again to do...whatever. I couldn't stake the house out, I couldn't watch you all 24-7, so I did what I could to help out. I knew you wouldn't accept my help, and I didn't know how to approach JaLea, since I never met her."

"So you give a gun to her grandmother?!" Isaiah yelled.

"You say that like she's eighty!" Isaac protested.

"It doesn't matter! It was stupid either way. I'm sure my mama told you what JaLea's grandma went through. She just got home. Are you stupid-"

"Enough!" Kim shouted. Isaiah leaned back into the cushion. "It was my idea." My eyes got wide as hell. *Kim's* idea?

"*Mama*?" Isaiah's voice came out almost in a whine. "You do know what happened last night, right?" he asked. Kim nodded and he groaned. "Why put her in that predicament?"

"Would you rather the nurse called and told you that he did something to one of them? Or maybe not get a call at all. What if you just went home to find them dead?" I couldn't speak. I was still dumbfounded that it was *Kim's* idea to give my G-mama a gun.

"How did you know? How did y'all get wind that something was about to happen? *We* didn't even know until a day ago," I asked.

"Well…" Kim looked at Isaac, who looked to his right. I followed their gaze to Tasha and shook my head and laughed.

"Y'all are kidding, right?" They were quiet.

"I admit," Tasha started talking to me and I rolled my eyes almost out of reflex. "I was all for revenge. You wouldn't listen to anything I had to say, sis said you didn't want any of my letters. I tried to be there for you and just sent me away to rot."

"What the hell?! You set my mama up and *you* are mad at *me*? All that time you knew exactly who it was that killed her and you let me drive myself crazy. You let my grandmamma think all hope was lost! You weren't *there* for me!"

"I always loved you like a daughter, JaLea-"
"Bullshit!"

"I'm not lying! Look me in my eyes and you'll see I'm not lying!" It looked like she was just about to lose it. "When Kim told me what happened to you-" she closed her eyes and put her head in her hands. "I was in there havin' a nervous breakdown. I tried to call you once, but you wouldn't accept. Then when that asshole started to visit me again, he seemed desperate. Looked like somebody had beat the shit outta him." I laughed to myself. "I knew he still trusted me. I figured it was my way in."

"Way into what?" Isaiah asked.

"Into his head. I knew I could get him to tell me damn near his every move. So maybe I could warn y'all. He was excited about me gettin' out. Said it would be much easier to work wit' me when I got out. At first I kept it to myself because I didn't want my sister in it, but then he started gettin' amped, said he didn't wanna wait for me. He started talkin' about gettin' in the house and doin' stuff to yo' granny. I couldn't just keep my mouth shut no more. I had to say somethin' to her."

"It was the only thing we could come up with," Kim added.

"The *only* thing?" I asked, skeptical.

"Yes, JaLea. Desperate times call for desperate measures. Isaiah told me before that you don't want guns in the house and I didn't want to have you mad at him. Your granny is there with the nurse most of the time. Two helpless women there alone-"

"My grandmama *killed* a man!"

"And if she hadn't had the gun, he would've killed *her*." Thinking about it made my stomach turn.

"And if I had been there alone?" I asked.

"His plan wasn't to physically hurt *you*," Tasha said.

"What?!" I jumped up. "I can't tell judging by all the days I spent in a coma!"

"Calm down! Can I finish?" Tasha yelled right back. I wanted to scratch her throat out.

"No because it sounds like you're protecting his ass!"

"And why the hell would I do that?"

"Really?!" I couldn't believe she would ask that! "Maybe because you been helping him all this time! You're the one who sent him to my house, who hooked him up wit' Theresa."

"Baby-" Isaiah tried to grab my arm but I yanked away from him.

"You helped him kill Terrell!"

"No I-" I was on her before she could finish her sentence. I relished every blow I landed until Isaiah and his dad pulled me off. I could hear Kim in the background muttering 'oh my God' over and over again. My eyes were trained on Tasha though as she grabbed her mouth. Blood seeped from her nose and bottom lip and I smiled at her. She nodded. "It's cool. I deserve that."

"That ain't all yo' ass deserve!"

"JaLea, *please*," Kim begged.

"Please what?!" I barked. "This is exactly what I was talking about, Kim! You having to choose sides and I'm sure it's gonna be your sister each and every time."

"I'm not taking sides! I don't want the two of you fighting!"

"Oh, you want me to just forgive her? Is that it? I'm not you! It was my mama-"

"JaLea-" Tasha cut in.

"What?!" I screamed.

"Please don't be mad at Kim. She's been cleanin' up after me for years because she feels obligated to. I know I did a lot of stupid shit, but I guarantee you that dude started in on you *way* before he contacted me. Let him tell it, he started watchin' you right after his brother got locked up. By the time he reached out to me, he already knew all types of stuff about you. He was the one who brought up Theresa because he knew she was on drugs. He already *knew* that! And keep in mind what I had to go through before I even said yes. What those women did to me in there." She shook her head like she was trying to shake the thought away. When Kim told me about everything Tasha was going through, I didn't give a damn. In fact, I thought it was funny. But standing there listening to her, I started to feel myself soften up. "I didn't *wanna* help him at first. After you never accepted my letters and after goin' through all that I went through, I just kinda fell in line with what he was doin'. I never thought he was gonna hurt you and I definitely didn't know he was the one who killed Terrell, until Kim told me. I swear to you I didn't! When I found out you were in the hospital, I took it so hard. I wanted to stick it to his ass, but I guess he thought I hated you as much as he did and that I was out for blood. It wasn't even like that. Broken windows and shit, that's what I signed up for. Not for anybody to get *physically* hurt. Especially not you." I stared at Tasha after she was done rambling. I wanted to still be pissed. I wanted to not believe a word Tasha was saying because it was what I was used to. I was so ready to confront her, go off on her, shut her out of my life and be done with it. I wasn't ready to hear her sob story and actually think she was telling the *truth*! Surprisingly, I did. I believed her.

My shoulders began to slump and I felt Isaiah loosen his grip on me, finally feeling that I was calm. I was searching my mind for something to say. I didn't wanna hug her. I wasn't there yet, but all eyes were on me, like I *needed* to say something. I opened my mouth, then closed it, unsure of how I was supposed to respond. Then, as if it felt that I was between a rock and a hard place, my phone started ringing. I didn't recognize the number, but I answered anyway.

"Hello?"

"Hello, is this JaLea Washington?" the man on the other end asked.

"Yes, it is," I answered. Tasha turned away and everybody else was staring at me with an attitude, like how dare you answer the phone right now.

"This is Officer Carnett at Southeast Correctional Institute." I went limp and Isaiah grabbed me under my arms to hold me.

"Who is it?" he demanded. I couldn't speak. The only other person I knew who was locked up was the bastard who killed my mama. I was so sure that Chris had heard his brother was murdered and somehow escaped. It was the only reason I could think that they'd be calling me.

"Yes," I didn't recognize the voice that came out of my mouth.

"Yes, ma'am I'm contacting you as a courtesy to inform you that Christopher Merritt was found in his cell a couple of hours ago, non-responsive. He appears to have committed suicide."

EPILOGUE

"Rell! Don't run over Iesha!" I yelled as he zoomed past his sister.

"Chill, baby." Isaiah wrapped his arm around me as we watched Iesha teeter around the park. We had been so happy when we found out we were pregnant, and overjoyed when we found out we were having a girl. Isaiah had long considered Lil Rell his son, but to see his own child be brought into the world was something special that couldn't be topped by much of anything. I'd always love Terrell, but Isaiah had helped complete my heart again. He had helped put the broken pieces together and make me whole, which I thought I'd never be.

"He's four and she's only one," I protested. "He's gon' end up knocking her lil' yellow, bow-legged behind down."

"They'll be okay," he laughed.

"Yea stop bein' so anal," Erika added. "I'm not scared he's gonna knock Tamika down."

"That's because yo' baby is a bully," I laughed and she punched me in the arm.

"Whatever. I'mma go see if yo' daddy finished the barbeque yet. I'm hungry as hell." I nodded as she walked away.

"That's all I'm sayin! When will the food be done?" Mesha complained from behind us at the picnic table. "We under a pavilion in the shade and it's still hot as hell. Whose idea was it to have this damn get-together in June *anyway*?" She shook her head.

"You know it was mine heffa!" I told her.

"Why are pregnant women always complaining?" Isaiah laughed.

"*Excuse you*?" Mesha asked him.

"Ain't she always complaining, babe?" he asked me. "Where did Samir go while you over here bothering us?" I got up, trying to sneak away. "Oh you just gon' leave like that?" he asked.

"I'm not getting' in that at all," I laughed.

"Oh, you betta get in it if you wanna be a God-mama in three months!" Mesha yelled after me. "Lil Diva said bring her back a hot dog!" I shook my head at her and walked over to where my dad was cooking. His fiancé, Victoria, clung to him. They were so cute together. When I first met her at my dad's right after we found out about Theresa, I wasn't sold on her. She was gorgeous, loving, and supportive and she cared about my dad so much. He had already been on the road to recovery, but she went out of her way to help breath life back into him. She loved him dearly and that made me love her.

"Hey, y'all," I greeted them. "Dad, everybody is wondering when you're gonna bless us with some meat."

"It's comin', sweetie," he grinned, showing off his new pearly whites. They weren't his, but if you didn't know his back story, you'd never guess. Thanks to Victoria, he had landed a job with Wells Fargo, they had a nice lil' house in North County and were doing pretty well for themselves. I was beyond proud of how far he'd come. He and Victoria even kept the kids sometimes. "Where's my grandbabies?" he asked. I pointed in the direction of Isaiah and Mesha.

"Still over there runnin' in circles," I told him. "I need you to speed up that meat. I'm gettin' hungry," I teased.

"You yellin' at him?" Veronica jumped in. "Don't make me have to get wit'chu," she joked.

"I can take you," I told her.

"Yea, whatever." She waved her hand at me and I stuck my tongue out at her. I made my rounds, circling over to where G-mama was talking to the photographer. They were leaning against the side of the gazebo just laughing it up. Mr. Charles was seated at the table nearest them, reading a magazine.

"Do you do anything else besides read?" I asked him.

"It's the best past time there is," he winked at me. Strange how Theresa's death had brought us together. As the years passed, we became more and more cordial with each other, eventually, dare I say it, being nice to one another. "Besides, I can buy more books now that I don't have to pay to take care of her." He jerked his head towards G-mama.

"Kiss my ass Charles, okay." She stayed goin' off.

"G-mama!" I scolded. She was almost worse than Mesha.

"What? You betta tell him to leave me alone." She rolled her eyes and went back to her conversation. I grabbed her arm and pulled her away. "I'mma whoop you in *two* minutes if you don't let me go."

"G-mama! He looks thirty!" I said, glaring at the photographer.

"I know," she purred.

"Really? About two years older than your own *granddaughter*?"

"Since you in my business, I ain't had none since January-"

"Where did you get some from in January?" I was outdone with her!

"You remember the young guy-"

"Nevermind!" I held my hand up. "Go on back to yo' conversation." I hurried away. The last thing I needed in life was mental pictures.

"*Renig!*" Tasha yelled as I walked up to the picnic table where she, Kim, Isaac, and his other two kids were. Isaiah had made his way over to the table and was standing behind his dad. It was uncanny how much he looked like his younger brother and sister, even though they had different mothers. Kim was sitting comfortably on Isaac's lap. I had met Isaiah's siblings while I was pregnant with Iesha. I assumed at first that he had only brought them around since they were about to have a niece, but shortly after, I started seeing Isaac all the time. He was popping up at get-togethers, and family dinners, and he'd be over at Kim's all hours of the night. I didn't ask any questions, and Kim didn't offer any answers. I had long since realized that Kim would let you know what she wanted you to know when she wanted you to know it. All she'd shared with Isaiah was that she and his dad were working on *them*, whatever that meant. My nosey ass wanted to know what happened between him and his wife, and Isaiah wasn't comfortable asking. I tried to get him to ask his siblings, but he wasn't havin' it. He wanted to build their relationship as siblings before he started getting all in their business. He assumed eventually it would come out. I joked with him about how long it took for me to even find out his dad existed.

"Renig how?" Isaac yelled flipping through his books. Tasha snapped cards on the table like only a true Spades player could, and we all laughed.

"Yea, baby, you messed up," Kim told him. It was so good to see her happy and not lonely. I couldn't bear her cooped up in the house with Tasha all day. We had all tried to intervene with Tasha. After being locked up so for so long, she had that initial shock of being back in society with no one telling her what to do or when and how to do it. She had to get used to eating and sleeping on her own schedule, and she was even uncomfortable in the bed in Kim's guest room for a while. Eventually, she did get a job and a small studio apartment. It was a struggle to get her to where she was, but I was there with Kim every step of the way. I truly did believe she had remorse for what she had done, to me and my mama. She had apologized over and over again, and Kim had saved the letters she had written me just in case I decided to read them one day. They had brought tears to my eyes. The sadness she had for playing part in losing her best friend was clear. And she more than made up for it. Even though I didn't like the way she, Kim, and Isaac had gone about it, they got the job done. There was no telling what kind of havoc Derrick would've let loose in the days to come. He needed to be put down like the damn rabid dog he was.

    When I got the call from the jail that Chris had committed suicide, I couldn't believe the words. I heard them, but for the life of me, I had to have him repeat it three times before Isaiah finally took the phone from me to find out what was going on. First of kin had to be contacted about Derrick's death, and, since Chris was the only family he had, he was the one informed. They were everything to each other, which was why Derrick was so damn gung-ho on making my life living hell. When they told Chris, he flipped out. He started fighting guards and throwing a fit. A few hours later, they found him in his cell. He had hung himself from the bars on his window and left a letter saying: *Fuck it. Who else do I have to live for?* I thought it tacky to celebrate, but we did enjoy the following days of living without fear, once the shock wore off. I had gone to visit my mama, letting her know her family was safe and she could finally rest easy.

    "Okay y'all, my new boo ready to take the pictures now!" G-mama yelled out. I rolled my eyes while everybody else laughed. She was a piece of work. We all piled up beside the pavilion, joking and cheesing, making it take forever to get a decent picture. As I stood, Isaiah on one side with Lil Rell hugging his leg, my dad on the other with my daughter resting on his hip, I couldn't help but think about how my life was near perfect in my eyes. It was amazing how all of us, me, Isaiah, his dad, G-mama, Kim, Tasha, my dad and his woman, Mesha, Samir and even Erika and Mr. Charles were able to coexist. It was a far cry from a couple of years before. I had been at the lowest of lows, so focused on revenge that, at times, I had neglected the people who loved me, including Isaiah and even my son. Now I had a full family. Weird as it may look to many people, we were as close as family could get. We had all been through hell and back together, and somehow, *finally*, after all the drama and bullshit, the demons and secrets and drugs and death we had to endure, we were able to come out on top. The sun was shining on us. I'd like to think it was my mama smiling down on everybody. Either way, I was finally happy. I was finally free.

Made in the USA
Lexington, KY
31 May 2017